zac

&

mia

by A. J. BETTS

Houghton Mifflin Harcourt
Boston   New York

www.hmhco.com

Text set in Aldus LT Std.

Library of Congress Cataloging-in-Publication Data
Betts, A. J., 1975–
Zac and Mia / A. J. Betts.
p. cm.
Originally published in Australia by Text Publishing in 2013.
Summary: "The last person Zac expects in the room next door is a girl like Mia, angry and feisty with questionable taste in music. In the real world, he wouldn't—couldn't—be friends with her. In the hospital different rules apply, and what begins as a knock on the wall leads to a note—then a friendship neither of them sees coming." —Provided by publisher
ISBN 978-0-544-33164-8
[1. Friendship—Fiction. 2. Cancer—Fiction.] I. Title.
PZ7.B46638Zac 2014
[Fic]—dc23
2013050126

Manufactured in the United States of America
DOC 10 9 8 7 6 5 4
4500521042

For the Zacs and Mias. The real ones.

PART ONE
Zac

1
Zac

A newbie arrives next door. From this side of the wall I hear the shuffle of feet, unsure of where to stand. I hear Nina going through the arrival instructions in that buoyant air hostess way, as if this "flight" will go smoothly, no need to pull the emergency exit lever. Just relax and enjoy the service. Nina has the kind of voice you believe.

She'll be saying, *This remote is for your bed. See? You can tilt it here, or recline it with this button. See? You try.*

Ten months ago, Nina explained these things to me. It was a Tuesday. Plucked from a math class in period two, I was bustled into the car with Mum and an overnight bag. On the five-hour drive north to Perth, Mum used words like "precautions" and "standard testing." But I knew then, of course. I'd been tired and sick for ages. I knew.

I was still wearing my school uniform when Nina led me into Room 6 and showed me how to use the bed remote, the TV remote, and the internal phone. With a flick of her wrist she demonstrated how to tick the boxes on the blue menu card:

breakfast, morning tea, lunch, afternoon tea, dinner. I was glad Mum was paying attention, because all I could think about was the heaviness of my school bag and the English essay that was due the next day, the one I'd gotten an extension for already. I do remember the clip Nina had in her hair, though. It was a ladybug with six indented spots. Funny how the brain does things like that. Your whole world is getting sucked up and tossed around and the best you can do is fixate on something small and unexpected. The ladybug seemed out of place, but like a piece of junk in the ocean it was something, at least, to cling to.

I can recite the nurses' welcoming spiel by heart these days. *If you get cold, there are blankets in here*, Nina will be saying. I wonder what hair clip she's wearing today.

"So," says Mum, as casually as she can. "A new arrival."

And I know that she loves it and hates it. Loves it because there's someone new to meet and greet. Hates it because this shouldn't be wished on anyone.

"When did we last get a new one?" Mum recalls names. "Mario, prostate; Sarah, bowel; Prav, bladder; Carl's colon; Annabelle . . . what was she?"

They've all been oldies over sixty, well entrenched in their cycles. There was nothing new or exciting about any of them.

A nurse darts past the round window in my door—Nina. Something yellow's in her hair. It could be a chicken. I wonder if she has to go to the kids' section of stores to buy them. In the real world, it'd be weird for a twenty-eight-year-old woman to wear plastic animals in her hair, wouldn't it? But in here, it kind of makes sense.

My circular view of the corridor returns to normal: a white

wall and two-thirds of the VISITORS, IF YOU HAVE A COUGH OR COLD, PLEASE STAY AWAY sign.

Mum mutes the TV with the remote and shifts in her chair. Hoping to pick up vital audio clues, she turns her head so her good ear is nearest the wall. When she tucks her hair behind her ear, I see there's more gray than there used to be.

"Mum—"

"Shhh." She leans closer.

At this point, the standard sequence is as follows: The new patient's "significant other" comments on the view, the bed, and the size of the bathroom. The patient agrees. There's the flicking through the six TV channels, then a switching off. Often, there's nervous laughter at the gray stack of disposable urinals and bedpans, prompted by the naive belief the patient will never be weak enough or desperate enough to use them.

And then there's a stretch of silence that follows their gaze from one white wall—with its plugs and label-makered labels and holes for things they can't even imagine yet—to the other. They track the walls, north to south, east to west, before they sag with the knowledge that this has become real, that treatment will start tomorrow, and this bed will become home for several days, on again, off again, in well-planned cycles for however many months or years it'll take to beat this thing, and there is no emergency exit lever. Then the significant other will say, *Oh, well, it's not so bad. Oh, look, you can see the city from here. Look.*

Sometime later, after unpacking clothes and trying out the cafeteria's coffee for the first time, the new person inevitably crawls into bed with two magazines and the knowledge that this isn't a flight after all, but a cruise, and their room is a cabin beneath the water's surface, where land is something only to dream of.

But whoever is in Room 2 isn't following the standard sequence of action. There's a loud thump of a bag and that's it. There's no unzipping. There's no click-clacking of coat hangers at the back of the wardrobe, no rattling of toiletries in the top drawer. Worse, there's no soothing verbal exchange.

Mum turns to me. "I should go say hi."

"Only because you're losing," I say, trying to buy the new patient some time. Mum's only behind by five points and admittedly we're both having a crap round. My best word has been BOGAN, which caused some debate. Hers was GLUM, which is pretty sad.

Mum lays out BOOT and adds six points to her score. "Nina didn't mention there was a new admission."

She says this without irony, as if she actually expects to be told of the comings and goings of patients on Ward 7G. Mum's been here so long, she's forgotten she belongs somewhere else.

"It's too soon."

"Just a tea . . ."

My mother: the Unofficial Welcoming Committee of the oncology ward. The maker of calming teas, and the bringer of cafeteria scones with individual portions of plum jam. The self-appointed sounding board for patients' families.

"Finish the game," I tell her.

"But what if they're alone? Like what's-his-name? Remember him?"

"Maybe they *want* to be on their own." Isn't that normal? To want to be alone sometimes?

"Shush!"

Then I hear it too. I can't make out the words at first—there's a plaster wall between us, about six centimeters I guess—but I hear a simmering of sounds.

"Two women," Mum says, her hazel eyes dilating. Her mouth twists as she listens to the s's and t's that spit and hiss. "One is older than the other."

"Stop snooping," I tell her, but it's not as if we can help it. The voices are growing louder, words firing like projectiles: *Shouldn't! Stop! Don't! Wouldn't!*

"What is going *on* in there?" Mum asks, and I offer her my empty glass to press, spy-like, against the wall.

"Don't be a smartass," she says, and then, "That doesn't actually work, does it?"

It's not as if my family doesn't fight. There were times, years ago, when Mum and Bec would go right off. They'd be on their feet, vicious as rottweilers. Dad and Evan would back out of the house, escaping to the olive farm, where blistering voices couldn't follow, but I'd often stay on the veranda, not trusting them to be left alone.

The fights lost their intensity once Bec turned eighteen. It helped that she moved into the old house next door, which was once used for workers. She's twenty-two now and pregnant, and she and Mum are close. They're still as stubborn as hell, but they've learned how to laugh at each other.

There's no laughing in Room 2. The voices sound dangerous. There's swearing—then a door shuts. It doesn't slam, because all the doors are spring-loaded, closing with a controlled, unsatisfying *whoosh*. Then footsteps rush the corridor. A woman's head flashes past my window. She's short—her head skims the bottom edge. She's wearing brown-rimmed glasses and a tortoiseshell claw that grips most of her sandy hair. Her right hand clutches the back of her neck.

Beside me, Mum is all meerkat. Her attention twitches from the door to the wall, then to me. After twenty days in Room 1, she's forgotten that out in the real world people get pissed off, that tempers are short, like at school, where kids arc up after getting bumped in the lunch line. She's forgotten about egos and rage.

Mum readies herself to launch into action: to follow that woman and offer tea, date scones, and a shoulder to lean on.

"Mum."

"Yes?"

"Save the pep talk for tomorrow."

"You think?"

What I think is that they'll both need more than Mum's counsel. They'll need alcohol, probably. Five milligrams of Valium, perhaps.

I lay down NOSY, snapping the squares onto the board, but Mum doesn't take the bait.

"Why would anyone argue like that? In a cancer ward? Surely they'd just—"

As if through a megaphone, a voice comes booming through the wall.

"What . . . on . . . earth . . . ?"

Then a beat kicks in that jolts us both. Mum's letters clatter to the floor.

Music, of sorts, is invading my room at a level previously unknown on Ward 7G. The new girl must have brought her own speakers and lumped them on the shelf above the bed, facing the wall, then cranked them right up to the max. Some singer howls through the plaster. Doesn't she know it's *our* wall?

Mum's sprawled on all fours, crawling under my bed to retrieve her seven letters, while the room throbs with electropop *ass-squeezing* and *wanting it bad*. I've heard the song before, maybe a year or two ago.

When Mum gets up off the floor, she's holding a bonus T and X, a strawberry lip balm, and a Mintie.

"Who's the singer?" Mum asks.

"How would *I* know?" It's whiny and it's an assault on my senses.

"It's like a nightclub in here," she says.

"Since when have you been in a nightclub?"

Mum raises an eyebrow as she unwraps the Mintie. To be fair, I haven't been in a nightclub either, so neither of us is qualified to make comparisons. The noise level is probably more blue-light disco, but it's a shock for two people who've spent so long in a quiet, controlled room with conservative neighbors.

"Is it Cher? I liked Cher . . ."

I'm not up to speed on female singers with single names. Rihanna? Beyoncé? Pink? Painful lyrics pound their way through the wall.

Then it hits me. The newbie's gone Gaga. The girl's got cancer *and* bad taste?

"Or is it Madonna?"

"Are you still playing or what?" I say, intersecting BOOT with KNOB. The song is banging on about riding on a *disco stick*. Seriously?

Mum finally pops the Mintie into her mouth. "It must

be a young one," she says softly. Young ones upset her more than old ones. "Such a shame." Then she turns to me and is reminded that, yes, I'm a young one too. She looks down at her hand of disjointed letters, as if trying to compose a word that could make sense of this.

I know what she's thinking. Damn it, I've come to know her too well.

"They must be good speakers, don't you think?" she says.

"What?"

"We should have brought your speakers from home, shouldn't we? Or bought some. I could go shopping tomorrow."

"Go steal hers."

"She's upset."

"That song is destroying my white blood cell count."

I'm only half joking.

The song ends, but there's no justice, because it starts again. The *same song*. Honestly, Lady freaking Gaga? At this volume?

"It's your turn." Mum places BOARD carefully on the . . . board. Then she plucks another four letters from the bag as if everything is normal and we're not being aurally abused.

"The song's on *repeat*," I say, unnecessarily. "Can you ask her to stop?"

"Zac, she's new."

"We were all new once. It's no excuse for . . . *that*. There's got to be a law. A patient code of ethics."

"Actually, I don't mind it." Mum nods her head as proof. Bopping, I believe it's called.

I look into my lap at the T F J P Q R S. I don't even have a vowel.

I give up. I can't think; don't want to. I've had enough of this song, now playing for the third time in a row. I try to suffocate myself with a pillow.

"Do you want a tea?" Mum asks.

I don't want tea—I *never* want tea—but I nod so I can be alone for a few minutes, or an hour, if she tracks down the newbie's significant other and performs emergency scone therapy in the patients' lounge.

I hear water running as Mum follows the hand-washing instructions conscientiously.

"I won't be long."

"Go!" I say. "Save yourself."

When the door closes behind her, I release the pillow. I slide my Scrabble letters into the box and recline my bed to horizontal. I'm finally granted precious mother-free time and it's ruined by *this*. The song begins for the fourth time.

How is it possible that Room 1 can be such an effective sanctuary from the germs of the outside world, but so pathetic at protecting me from the hazards of shit music?

I can't hear the girl—I can't hear anything but that song—but I reckon she's lying on her bed, mouthing the lyrics, while I'm doing my best to ignore them.

Room 2 is pretty much identical to mine. I know; I've stayed there before. They have the same wardrobe, same bathroom, same paint and blinds. Everything is in duplicate, but as a mirror image. If looked at from above, the bed headboards would appear to back onto each other, separated only by the six-centimeter width of this wall.

If she's lying on her bed right now, we are practically head-to-head.

Farther down the corridor, there are six other single rooms, then eight twin-bedders. I've been in each of them. When I was diagnosed the first time in February, I became a frequent flyer for six months, moving through cycles of induction, consolidation, intensification, and maintenance. At the end of each chemo cycle, Mum would drive us the five hundred kilometers back home, where I'd rest, get some strength, and make it to a day or two of school, even though my classmates were preparing for exams I wouldn't get to take. Then we'd yo-yo back to Perth, settling in to whichever room was free and bracing ourselves for the next hit.

We both expected chemo to work. It didn't.

"If you can't zap it, swap it," Dr. Aneta had rallied when I relapsed. On a planner she highlighted a fluorescent yellow block from November 18 to December 22. *Zac Meier*, she printed. *Bone Marrow Transplant. Room 1.* The first eight or nine days would be to zap me again, she explained, ready for the transplant on "Day 0." The rest of the stay would be for strict isolation, to heal and graft in safety.

"Five weeks in the same room?" Shit, even high-security prisoners get more freedom than that.

She clicked the lid back onto the pen. "At least you'll be out in time for Christmas."

Before leukemia, I had enough trouble sitting in a room for two hours, let alone a whole day. Everything interesting happened outside: football, cricket, the beach, and the farm. Even at school, I'd always sit by the window so I could see what I was missing out on.

"Room One's got the best view," Dr. Aneta said, as if that could sweeten it. As if I had a choice.

The song ends and I hold my breath. For a moment, I hear only the predictable sounds: the whir of my drip, the hum of my bar fridge.

I wonder if the newbie is counting the squares on her ceiling for the first time. There are eighty-four, I could tell her. Eighty-four, just like mine. Or maybe she's already recounting them the opposite way, just to be sure.

• • •

Eighteen freaking times? Methotrexate is nothing—*this* is killing me.

The nurses are still in their weekly meeting, so there's no one to save me from this endless cycle of crap. Who would listen to a song eighteen times? Make it nineteen. Is this girl mental? Is she experimenting with a new form of therapy, trying to make her cancerous cells spontaneously self-destruct? Is there some Lady Gaga Miracle Cancer Cure I haven't heard of?

Old patients never do this kind of thing. They have respect. Admittedly, Bill can turn his radio up too loud for the dog races, but the volume only reaches mildly annoying, not all-consuming. Then there's Martha, whose high-pitched cackle is grating, but only when she's drinking rooibos tea.

It's not as if I can get up off this bed, walk out the door, and find a quiet broom closet to hide myself in. Thanks to Bone Marrow Transplant Protocol I'm stuck in this four-by-five-meter room. Twenty days down, fifteen to go—which is too long to be held hostage to the obsessive compulsions of a girl next door. All I can do is put my pillow over my head and hope she's got Hodgkin's lymphoma, with a one-day-a-month cycle. I can't contemplate the possibility of her being an AML or ALL. If she's getting a BMT, I'm legging it.

The song begins again, making it twenty — the number I decided would be my breaking point. I have to do something before my ears start to bleed.

A shout won't penetrate her Gaga-thon. How else can I communicate through a six-centimeter-thick wall?

I get up off the bed and notice my hands are bunched into fists. So I use one.

I knock. Politely at first, as if I'm a visitor to someone's house. I knock, hoping the message gets through.

No. It doesn't seem to.

I knock again, in sets of three, as insistent as a courier this time. *Knock knock knock.* Wait. *Knock knock knock.*

The song reaches the chorus I've come to hate so much. Worse, I now know all the lyrics.

I bang harder, like an annoyed brother locked out. My fist thumps every beat in time, banging them so loudly, she must be hearing them in stereo. The wall on her side has to be bouncing with the impact.

The music stops — success! — and so do I, noticing how easily skin has peeled from my red knuckles. I rub it away and realize I'm grinning.

Perhaps it's because this is the first contact I've had with anyone since I've been in this room. Nurses, doctors, and my mum don't count. The new girl is young — someone my age. My heart pounds with the effort. I'm dizzy with it. My room throbs. *Whir. Drip. Hum.*

Then, *tap,* the wall says back to me. *Tap.*

The tap isn't angry like the music had been or the words she'd shouted earlier. The tap is close. She must be near now, puzzled, a curious ear against the wall, as if listening for alien contact.

I crouch.

Knock, I reply to the wall, down lower this time.

Tap.

The wall sounds hollow. Is it?

Knock.

Tap.

Knock.

Tap tap? In the quiet, the tap is raw. I think it's a question.

Knock.

In the gaps in between, there's nothing but the whirring of my IV machine and the anticipation of the next cue. My quads ache as I wait. My feet feel cold on the linoleum.

Tap?

Knock.

It's clear neither of us knows Morse code, and yet something is being spoken. I wonder what she's trying to ask me.

Knock. Silence. *Knock.*

And I wonder what I'm saying.

Then that's it.

Whir. Hum. Buzz. Drip. Whir.

On my knees by the wall, I'm ashamed. I shouldn't have complained about her music on her first day of admission. There are too many things I don't know.

She doesn't tap and I don't knock.

I just kneel, imagining she's doing the same, six centimeters away.

2
Zac

I know that dual-flush buttons are good because they're environmentally friendly and all that, but sometimes they're confusing. Do I press the half flush or the full? Some days I need a button that's in between.

I stand thinking about this for too long. Again.

I wash my hands, amused by the reflection in the mirror. My head is bald, lumpy, and asymmetrical, but my eyebrows are thicker than before. I appear to be morphing into one of those creepy guys from *Guess Who.*

I leave the bathroom and return to the room, where Mum's opened the blinds and pulled the pink reclining chair into sitting. In the morning light, her bed hair resembles a bird's nest with wiry twigs of gray.

"Well, how was it?" she asks.

"What?"

"You know . . ."

How many times can a seventeen-year-old discuss his crap? With his mother? I reached the limit eighteen days ago. At least she doesn't say, *Have you opened your bowels?* the way the nurses do.

"How's *yours*, Mum?"

"I'm just asking."

"You want me to photograph it next time?" I maneuver myself and the IV pole past her. She whacks me gently with a pillow.

"You want me to keep a log book?"

"A *bog* book." Mum impresses herself with her wordplay.

Documenting my bowel movements—now *that* is an excellent use for the so-called diary that Patrick gave me. He thought I'd benefit from *expressing my emotional journey*, or something like that. Instead, I could use it as a bog log, plotting frequency and consistency. I could color code each page, drawing big brown pie charts with annotations.

"How about: *Dear Diary, it's December ninth, twelve days post-transplant. Semi-diarrhea. I chose the half flush.*"

"I don't think that's what the diary's for."

"Not poo and spew?"

"It's for your *feelings*." Having raised two boys and Bec, Mum knows better than to use the "f" word in earnest.

"December ninth. I *feel* . . . lighter."

She smiles. "See, that's better."

I don't need to write about crap. Of any kind.

I conquered toilet training at three years of age. I wasn't a prodigy, sure, but a solid student. From then on, toileting was supposed to remain a private thing behind a locked door, far from a mother's queries. Mum's job was to monitor other things, like the kind of food going into my mouth in the first place. And she had. She'd done a good job.

And then this. At my worst, Mum wasn't only asking about my output, she was witnessing it. I'd tell her to leave the bedpans alone, which she did, but she often stayed in the room when the nurses cleaned me up or washed me down, even if she was pretending to do crosswords. I'd become a baby all over again, but with testosterone and pubic hair and nurses sponging me in shifts. Sometimes I was so out of it, I couldn't get embarrassed.

Before they could give me new marrow on "Day 0," they had to take me close to death. Five days of four chemo drugs, then three days of total-body irradiation. I felt as if a truck had run over me. Then reversed, tipped sideways, and landed on top of me. There was nothing to do but be pinned underneath. Breathing was hard work. Controlling my sphincter was beyond me.

I can handle that end of things myself now. Post-transplant, my symptoms are down to occasional vomiting, mouth ulcers, and dubious turds. To be honest, going to the bathroom has become one of my favorite pastimes. For ten minutes or so, no one's watching or prying or probing. I can just sit and think about things. It's not up there with solving world poverty, but it's an achievement. It's progress.

Mum closes her *Woman's Day* and gapes at me. "Have you been squeezing that zit?"

"I didn't touch it."

She's got a paranoia that I could trigger a massive explosion of pus and blood too powerful to be fixed by my measly platelets, ending with an emergency transfusion, which might not save my life. Death by pimple? Now *that* would be a stupid way to die. I wouldn't take the risk.

How is it fair that I can have leukemia *and* zits? If my hair grows back red, I'll be really pissed. My brother Evan's a redhead, but he dyes his hair in secret. He thinks no one can tell.

"So what do you want to do today?" Mum asks.

"Go base jumping?"

"We could play CUD."

Mum makes me laugh out loud, whether she means to or not. "COD," I correct her. "As in Call of Duty. And no, not really." All she does is camp around, then shriek when killed, using made-up swear words like *Fff . . . irewood* and *Shh . . . ipwreck*. Mum's not cut out for armed combat.

"So what do you want to do?"

"Breathe. Eat. Sleep. Repeat."

She pokes me. "Come on, Zac, you don't want to be *bored*."

My mother: Activities Coordinator, Unofficial Welcoming Committee, Diarrhea Detective, and Happiness Police. She ricochets from one role to the next, plugging gaps, swapping props, prodding, checking, *doing*.

I sense her antennae twitching, seeking out signs of melancholy. We both know there's a whole squad of reinforcements on standby: Patrick the psychologist, art therapists, teen mentors, Prozac, and, if desperate, clown doctors called over from the children's hospital.

"Do we need to use the 'f' word?"

"Fuck no."

She laughs. "Then help me do the puzzle from today's paper. Ooh, look, we need thirty words to get to genius."

The "f" word troubles me, but it's Mum's feelings I'm worried about, not my own.

"Mum, go home."

"Zac—"

"You don't have to stay. Anymore. I'm getting better."

It's true. Days Minus 9 to Minus 1 were hell. Day 0 was an anticlimax. Days 1 to 3 I can't recall, 4 to 8 were foul, 9 to 11 were uncomfortable, and now, twelve days after transplant, I'm starting to feel human again. I can handle this.

"I know," she says predictably, turning a page of her magazine. "But I like it here."

It's bullshit and we both know it. Mum's not a four-wall kind of woman. As long as I can remember, she's always had a straw hat and a sheen of sweat. She's hazel eyes and sun spots. She's greens and browns and oranges. She's a pair of pruning shears in hand. She's soil and pumpkins. She'd rather be picking pears or fertilizing olive trees than stuck in this room, with its pink reclining chair. More than anything, she's my dad's soul mate, though she won't go home when I ask her—even when I beg her.

My room has two windows. There's the small round one in the door that looks into the corridor, and there's the large rectangular one that looks out over the hospital entrance, parking lot, and nearby suburbs. That's the one she sits beside most days, like a flower tracking the sun.

"List three things you like about the hospital. Apart from the puzzles and gossip."

"I did like my son's company . . . once."

"Just go home."

After my first diagnosis, the whole family would drive up to Perth for each round of chemo. Mum, Dad, Bec, and Evan would stay in a motel room three blocks away, visiting each morning with games and magazines and more conversation than I could follow. Dad was bigger and louder than usual. He'd make jokes with Bec, as if the two of them had suddenly formed a slapstick comedy duo. Mum would shake her head in mock disapproval, while Evan hung back, eyeing the drips and nurses with suspicion. "Hospitals make me sick," I heard him say once. "The smell . . ." I didn't blame him—he didn't belong here either. At least he was honest about it.

Then each time they left in the evening, I would stand at the rectangular window and watch my small family trudge back to their motel. Dad would hold Mum's hand. Seven stories down, each of them looked sadder than they should have, especially Dad. To be honest, their visits made me feel worse, and this time I made Mum promise to keep them all away. Fortunately, Bone Marrow Transplant Protocol forbids more than one official visitor at a time, so Mum nominated herself. The only catch is, she never leaves.

"They don't need me at home. Bec's got the store under control. The pruning's been done so the men have it easy."

"But Dad—"

"Can look after himself."

"You know what I mean."

"I'm your mother," she reminds me, as if she's taken a vow to love and to cherish, to protect and to irritate, in sickness and in health (but especially in sickness), as long as we both shall live.

And with military focus, she begins the daily word puzzle from the newspaper. Mum approaches it as though something bigger could be at stake, as if our success with it would bring about a success in my treatment. Through the course of the day, as Nina, Patrick, Simone, Suzanne, and Linda enter and exit the room for various offerings and takings, obscure words are added until we reach thirty. Mum is over the moon and writes on the calendar under December ninth: *Genius!*

And that's why I agree to do the word puzzle, and Scrabble and "CUD" and every other activity she suggests. I do it to see the confidence in Mum's handwriting. Genius. Another success; another day passed.

It's during the six o'clock news that I realize I'm being watched.

Someone in the corridor is peering through my round window. She's young, maybe sixteen or seventeen, with big eyes, dark eyeliner, and thick brown hair that probably rolls on past her shoulders, farther down than I can see.

She's not a nurse, though. She's someone like me and I feel her eyes latch fiercely to mine.

I can't pull free. She's stunning.

Then I blink and she's gone.

Strange. She didn't look like a girly-pop lover. Not that Lady Gaga's been played again. Since she turned it off two days ago, all I've heard from Room 2 has been occasional arguing—the mother, I'm guessing, and the girl—followed by the predictable *whoosh* of the door. There hasn't been a trace of music or television or anything else.

Is that my fault? Because I knocked?

Mum and I watch the news, but right now it's not the outside world that interests me.

3
Zac

Status: **Need new tunes in here. Suggestions??**

"I need new tunes," I tell Mum after four rounds of Mario Kart and a torturous half-hour of *Ready, Steady, Cook*. With my taste buds screwed up from chemo I've lost any interest in food, so watching so-called celebrity chefs prance about with artichoke hearts has no appeal. Mum, however, considers it compulsory viewing. "I know my iPod playlist by heart."

"You want me to go to the music store?"

It's perfect: sending Mum on a CD-buying mission will give me at least an hour solo.

"Only if you have time . . ."

Mum finds her purse and smudges on lip-gloss. She washes her hands again and checks her face in the mirror.

"What should I get?"

"Ask the store. Tell them it's for a seventeen-year-old. *Male*."

She shakes her head. "No way. Write down some titles."

Thanks to Facebook, I suddenly have a list of sixty-seven recommended albums. My one status update led to a barrage of suggestions, many of them sugar-coated.

Skrillex! Get better Zac

I'll send you the latest Rubens and Of Monsters and Men. Proud of you bro, love Bec

---

Macklemore & ryan Lewis. Can't hold us ;-) take it easy Helga

---

Cancer is a Facebook friend magnet. According to my home page, I'm more popular than ever. In the old days, people would have prayed for each other—now they "like" and comment as if they're going for a world record. I'm not knocking it, but how can I choose a couple of albums out of sixty-seven?

"Surprise me," I tell Mum. "If they're crap, you can always swap them tomorrow."

This is genius. I could have Mum back and forth between here and the music store for the remainder of my admission, giving me valuable hours of freedom and her some much-needed exercise. Finally, my chemo-brain is starting to clear. I hope she never learns about iTunes.

Mum dries her hands with a paper towel. "We *could* do with more ice cream . . ."

And with a wave, she's gone.

Halle-bloody-freaking-lujah.

Whir. Buzz. Hum. Drip.

I throw off the sheet and step onto the linoleum.

It's the new girl's fourth day in. From what I hear—and don't hear—she's still alone. Her mum visits in the mornings but never stays for long. She doesn't sleep overnight the way mine does.

This morning I heard the clack of coat hangers in the girl's wardrobe. After four days, she was finally unpacking her clothes. It sounded like surrender.

She'll have a port in, below her collarbone. It'll be raised and numb from surgery. The nurses would have needled it already and she wouldn't have felt a thing. She won't be nauseous from chemo yet. Depending on which drugs she's getting, maybe she never will. She'll only be here for another three days, then home for five, before her next cycle—that's what Nina told Mum. The girl's got osteosarcoma.

Gender: Female
Age: 17
Location: Lower leg
Stage: Localized

Shit, if I were her I wouldn't be sulking. Her stats are awesome. Hasn't she Googled them? Doesn't she know how lucky she is?

Suck it up, I want to say. *You'll be home soon. Play your crappy music and count down the days.*

But the song she's playing now is more hip-hop than girly-pop. I push my IV pole closer, hoping to make out the lyrics.

With one ear pressed to the wall, I keep a check on my round window, not wanting to give anyone the wrong idea. Nurses walk indifferently past, as does a guy with a hat. He's younger than the typical visitor. He's carrying a helium balloon with a small white bear.

I hear him enter Room 2. He walks to the window side of her bed, I think. I can't understand all of his words. They come less often than the girl's, whose voice sounds lighter than ever, as bubbly as a soft drink. I wonder what he says to make this happen.

"Gross, take it off," she laughs, and I guess he's doing what all dickheads have done before him: using a cardboard bedpan as a hat. It's so obvious, I can't believe she falls for it.

He recites tomorrow's menu options from the blue card and helps her tick the boxes. I hear him describe a party she missed, and how Shay and Chloe had asked about her.

"Don't tell them—"

"I didn't."

"Good. I'll be out of here soon."

"What's that?" His voice is nearer to our wall. I imagine him touching the lump beneath her collarbone.

"It's a port."

"Freaky. Does it hurt?"

"No. Yeah."

"Will it leave a scar?"

It's ages before she cries. I hear each gasp and each long interval between.

"Hey . . . Hey. You said you'll be fixed soon, yeah?"

"Yeah."

"So don't cry."

He leaves soon after. When he cruises past my door, his brow is crinkled in a way that reminds me of my brother, Evan, keen to be elsewhere.

Whir, drip, hum, my room says.

Room 2 says nothing. Her silence is sadder than ever, and it pulls me in.

I crouch down and knock on our wall. How else can I speak to her?

I knock three times. My knuckles say, *Go on — put some music on. Put it on repeat, if you want. I can handle it.*

But I'm left unanswered.

"What are you doing, Zac?" Nina's beside me.

"I dropped . . . the letter Q."

"And how does a Q sound?" The clip in Nina's hair is a possum. It seems to be smirking too.

When I stand, I bang my head on the IV pump.

"I've got your meds." She rattles the container. "But perhaps you need something . . . stronger?"

I'm lightheaded when I say, "Go tell the newbie to play Lady Gaga."

"Why?"

"Because I don't know Morse code and my message got lost in translation."

Nina sizes me up. "I never picked you as a Gaga guy."

"I know it's not a standard request," I say, flashing the grin that inexplicably works on her. "Just once. For me?"

I spy the diary beside my bed, fling it open, and tear out a blank page. I write:

Play Gaga.
I INSIST!
(Really!)

I wonder if capitals are too much. Or the exclamation marks. I consider drawing a smiley face to offset any traces of sarcasm.

"Why don't you download Lady Gaga from iTunes?"

"*I* don't want to hear Gaga," I whisper, pointing to the wall. "I want *her* to hear Gaga."

Nina folds the page carefully. "As you wish, Zac. Take your pills, huh?"

Nina pockets the note, then washes her hands for the compulsory thirty seconds. It feels more like sixty.

"Where's your mum?"

"At the store buying music."

"Lady Gaga?"

I snort. "As if."

"Of course. You're okay then? On your own?"

"Definitely." I nod and she leaves, both of us grinning.

• • •

Mum's got a good snore happening, the way she always does at three a.m. One of these mornings I should record her as proof. She reckons she doesn't snore—that she barely even sleeps— but I know the truth. When she's at her noisiest, I'm at my most awake.

It's not Mum's fault: it's the three a.m. curse. I wake up bursting, go for the third pee of the night, then can't get back to sleep.

Three is the worst hour. It's too dark, too bright, too late, too early. It's when the questions come, droning like flies, nudging me one by one until my mind's full of them.

Am I a bus driver? Addicted to late-night television shopping? A long-distance skier? A musician? A juggler?

It's 3:04 and I'm wondering who I am.

The marrow's German—the doctors were allowed to tell me that much. I've had German marrow for fourteen days, and though I'm not yet craving pretzels or beer or lederhosen, it doesn't mean I'm not changed in other ways. Alex and Matt have nicknamed me Helga, and it's caught on. Now the whole football team thinks it's hilarious that I could be part pretzel-baking, beer-swilling, braid-swinging Fräulein from Bavaria with massive *die Brust*.

But is it true? Could I be?

I try to catch myself being someone else.

I know it sounds like a B-grade thriller—*When Marrow Attacks!*—but if my own marrow's been wiped out of my bones and then replaced with a stranger's, shouldn't that change who I am? Isn't marrow where my cells are born, to bump their way through the bloodstream and to every part of me? So if the birthplace of my cells now stems from another human being, shouldn't this change everything?

I'm told I'm now 99.9 percent someone else. I'm told this is a good thing, but how can I know for sure? There's nothing in this room to test myself with. What if I now kick a football with the skill of a German beer wench? What if I've forgotten how to drive a pickup truck or ride an ATV? What if my body doesn't remember how to run? What if these things aren't stored in my head or muscles, but down deeper, in my marrow? What if . . .

what if all of this is just a waste of time and the leukemia comes back anyway?

At 3:07 I switch on the iPad, dim the brightness, and track my way through the maze of blogs and forums, safe from the prying eyes of Mum. Snoring in the recliner beside me, she's oblivious to my dirty secret.

In less than a second, Google tells me there are more than 742 million sites on cancer. Almost eight million are about leukemia; six million on acute myeloid leukemia. If I Google "cancer survival rate" there are more than eighteen million sites offering me numbers, odds, and percentages. I don't need to read them: I know most of the stats by heart.

On YouTube, the word *cancer* leads to 4.6 million videos. Of these, about 20,000 are from bone marrow transplant patients like me, stuck in isolation. Some are online right now. It may be 3:10 a.m. in Perth, but it's 7:10 a.m. in Auckland, 3:10 p.m. in Washington, D.C., and 8:10 p.m. in Dublin. The world is turning and thousands of people are awake, updating their posts on the bookmarked sites that I trawl through. I've come to know these people better than my mates. I can understand their feelings better than my own. Somehow, I feel like I'm intruding. Yet I watch their video uploads with my earbuds in. I track their treatment, their side effects and successes. And I keep a tally of the losses.

Then I hear the flush of the toilet next door.

The new girl and I have one thing in common, at least.

4
Zac

Fourteen days post-transplant and it's official. I am hideous.

I knew my face had puffed up—steroids will do that to you—but I hadn't realized how much. Either Nina has switched my bathroom mirror with one from the House of Mirrors, or my head has been replaced with a giant Rice Krispy.

Why hasn't anyone told me? Why have they been pussy-footing around the obvious deformity that is my head? Only two days ago Dr. Aneta called me a hottie, and I'd assumed she wasn't referring to my temperature. Nina was talking me up too, and took my photo with Mum's phone. Mum sent it to my sister, Bec, who posted it to my Facebook wall, causing a bombardment of two hundred compliments, including private messages from Clare Hill and Sienna Chapman. Sienna wrote she wants to "catch up" when I'm home, and Sienna wouldn't use those words lightly. Was she actually impressed, or was she blinded by charity? It happened in *Beauty and the Beast*, didn't it?

In my opinion, the only accurate comment came from Evan. *Nice pic, scrotum-face. Suits you.* Prick.

According to the bathroom mirror, I have no neck. Is it possible my German donor was, in fact, Augustus Gloop? Or has all the ice cream I've been eating gone straight to my chins?

The doctors say that it's good to put on fat after a transplant, that it helps the fight, or something like that. Well, it certainly doesn't help the ego, especially when the new girl keeps peeking through my window.

How is it fair that she gets to wander the ward freely, flaunting her glossy hair, perfect cheekbones, and single chin as she stares into other patients' rooms to judge them and their pasty, bloated heads, while I'm stuck in here being force-fed ice cream and lies, making a total fat fool of myself?

Which would explain why she hasn't replied to my handwritten note. Why would someone like her bother communicating with a bald Jabba the Hutt like me? Especially now that she's caught me playing Clue with my mother.

I know I shouldn't care what she thinks—this is temporary, after all—but what if she thinks this is me, the *real* me?

"Mum!"

"What?"

I point to my face and raise my eyebrows. At least, I think that's what I'm doing. "What breakfast cereal do I remind you of?"

"Stop ogling yourself and get back to bed. You have to guess if it was the candlestick or the rope."

"No."

"It was the candlestick." Mum snaps the board shut and stretches. "Is it afternoon tea time yet?"

We notice it at the same time: a folded piece of paper on the floor. I look at it, then at the door, which hasn't been opened in hours.

Mum walks over, picks it up, and sniffs it, as if her nose is trained to detect traces of contamination.

"Is it from Nina? I hope it's clean." She unfolds the paper and shows me the CD inside.

I launch myself to snatch it from her. The rush dizzies me; the surprise panics me. The page is blank. Why didn't she write something?

I flip the CD to read *Lady Gaga for Rm 1* scrawled in blue marker. The realization is sickening: the newbie not only pities me as a steroidal puffball, but she also believes I like girly-pop music. Next she'll be sending me CDs of Justin Bieber.

Oh, fuck, does she think I'm gay? Not that there's anything wrong with that . . .

"Pop it in the laptop." Mum levers the lid from the ice cream. "Let's listen."

Is my pasty face capable of blushing with humiliation? Would my red blood count be high enough to enable such a luxury?

I consider banging on our wall to set the girl straight: *I'm a 100 percent hetero, dirt-biking half-forward flank!*

But that would take a whole lot of knocking, and I don't want her to risk confusing it with *Thanks! Thanks heaps! I love Gaga more than life itself! Snaps for Gaga!*

Could she really believe she's indulging my audio and emotional needs? Or is there the slightest chance she's taking the piss out of me?

Mum's delight at seeing me pick up my diary is quickly destroyed by my violent tearing out of a page. She tries to appease me with a spoonful of pink ice cream.

"Go on. It's your favorite."

It's not, really.

I scribble:

> *Dear patient in Room 2.*
>
> *Thank you for your thoughtful present.*
>
> *Note: I am being <u>sarcastic!</u> You can't hear my voice, but believe me, there is much sarcasm. Try reading this aloud with the voice of Homer Simpson and you will hear . . .*

But when I read this back, it's not sarcastic at all. It's childish. And a bit crazed. So I scrunch this page and try another.

> *Dear neighbor*

No. Too religious.

> ~~*Dear*~~
>
> *To the girl in Room 2.*
>
> *I got your CD. Thanks. It's not my type though. But thanks. You go for gold. Knock yourself out.*
>
> *But not on repeat, surely, like you did that first day. Or that loud, I mean, within reason, you know. We're neighbors and the wall isn't that thick. Six or seven centimeters, so I've estimated. Maybe*

at certain hours. We could make some rules ... a
roster?

By this stage, Mum is making good work of a bowl of Nea-
politan ice cream while watching *Ready, Steady, Cook.*

I tap a fresh piece of paper with my pen. I can't remember
the last time I wrote an actual letter to someone, especially a
stranger. How do I get my point across without sounding like a
Nazi or a nut case?

I stare at the blank page and exhale. What am I trying to
say?

Hi. Thanks for the CD. You shouldn't have. It's not
what I meant ... But cheers. I'll add it to my col-
lection ...

There's a whole lot of white space staring back at me. What
do I say to a newbie who isn't coping?

There's a tile on your ceiling with a glow-in-
the-dark star on it. Have you noticed? My sister
Bec stuck heaps of them up there earlier in the
year. When I left, the ward manager made me peel
them off, but I kept one on. Is it still there? You've
got a good room. They say mine's the best but you
can see more of the football field from yours.
From the Bubble Boy in Room 1.
PS. Minor use of sarcasm earlier, in case you were
wondering.

PPS. Most TV shows make chemo worse, especially if they involve cooking, singing, dancing or Two and a Half Men. Seinfeld is the best sitcom for nausea.
PPPS. Don't order the chicken schnitzel on a Tuesday.

I replace the lid on the ballpoint pen and press the buzzer for Nina, who, after entering and washing, makes a beeline for my still-flowing drip. She frowns at me suspiciously, making her butterfly hair clip flutter. I pass her my folded note with *For Room 2* written across it before Mum can notice.

"Really? So that's all I am to you now?"

"What wouldn't you do for the hottest guy on the ward?" I say, hoping to catch her off-guard. She doesn't rebut so I point to my fat cheeks. "I mean, am I? Even with these?"

"Yes, Zac, you're still the fairest one of all. Anything else?"

"If I were a breakfast cereal, which one would I be?"

"In personality or appearance?" She doesn't miss a beat.

"Either."

"Lately? Verging on a Froot Loop."

She's not far wrong. I've been stuck in this room for twenty-five days and I'm getting pretty desperate for company. I don't mean my mum or the nurse or the psych or the PTs or anyone else who's paid to be here—I need interaction with people my own age, in real time. It's not enough to have online friends who sign in with bursts of exclamation marks, thumbs-up symbols, and smiley faces. I need something to remind me of the real world, uncensored and reckless.

I need a friend.

"Breakfast cereal?" Mum says hours later, after making up her pink bed, turning off the lights, and sliding under her blanket. "You're a strange one, Zac."

She's right. Ten days to go.

• • •

I've heard how cool children's oncology wards are, with huge lounges, rainbow-colored rooms, ukulele-playing clowns, and game rooms with drum kits and jukeboxes. Best of all, they're bombarded with professional basketball players and visiting soap stars bearing autographed gifts.

But because I was diagnosed at seventeen, I missed the cutoff and found myself in an adult hospital with white walls and a small cube for a television. On my first night in, I lay in bed and watched a documentary about the construction of NASA's new robot vehicle, the Curiosity rover. It was hard to stay focused amid the strange sounds and smells of the ward, and my nagging fear.

By the time I'd relapsed, the launch of Curiosity was all over the headlines. The night before my transplant, Mum and I watched the footage of the Atlas V shooting through the atmosphere, carrying its huge, robotic cargo. Even after we turned the TV off, I kept thinking about that robot hurtling through space. Inside it, scientific instruments were set to probe and dig into the surface of Mars, searching for the building blocks of life. If scientists can propel a robot 560 million kilometers away, I thought at the time, surely they can fix something as small as rogue blood cells in a body.

It's easy to go off on tangents here—there's nothing else

to do. I've become so bored that even the nurses' idiosyncrasies are interesting. Veronica, for instance, has huge hands, which are surprisingly nimble as she changes the sheets on my bed. Sitting in the pink chair, I admire her no-nonsense choreography. Her hospital corners are second to none.

"So, how's your morning been?" I ask her.

"Not so bad. You?"

"Standard. Have you been in Room Two yet?" Mum's currently using the visitors' showers down the corridor, so I have to take advantage of her absence.

Veronica nods.

"Did the girl say anything?"

Veronica snaps a sheet into place and shakes her head. She's accustomed to dealing with patients her own age or older, most of whom prattle on for hours about the temperature and/or quality of the hospital meals, not the status of girls-next-door. It's unusual to have two teenagers in an adult oncology ward, especially in adjoining rooms.

"Did she give you a message?"

"What do you mean by 'message'?"

Mum's face appears at my window. She'll be beginning her hand-washing routine, which leaves me with exactly thirty seconds. "Did she give you a note? About music . . . or *Seinfeld* or chicken schnitzel?"

Veronica makes a point of showing me her large, empty palms. "The only words that girl says are ones I won't be repeating. You opened your bowels?"

I close my eyes. "Yes. And urinated. Three times in the night, once this morning."

Veronica's pen scores sharp ticks on my chart. Can a man have no secrets? She checks my temperature. "Girls like that remind me why I had only boys," Veronica says, as if this were a clever choice on her part. "She is so . . . moody. Won't eat breakfast. Won't eat anything. Won't fill out the blue card. Won't open the curtains. And how she speaks to her mother . . ."

My own mother pushes through the door, carrying her towel and toiletries bag. "Morning, Veronica. He's pooed."

"Thanks, Mum. She knows." Everyone knows.

"See, boys, they have manners," Veronica continues. "Boys treat mothers with respect."

I peel myself from the chair and coerce my IV pole toward the bed, where I attempt to lever myself between impossibly taut sheets.

So starts Day 25: twenty-five in this room, fifteen post-transplant.

"Want to play COD, Mum?"

"Only if you want to die!" She catches herself too late.

I grin and shake my head. No chance.

• • •

Amid the gunfire and Mum's respawning for the fiftieth time, I hear something else. Something that doesn't belong to a Call of Duty Team Deathmatch.

It's the shouting of a real person. Two of them.

I turn down the volume.

"Who's snooping now?" says Mum.

"Shhh."

I hear the mother. "Why are you doing this to me?"

It's the *me* that jars most. Significant others are supposed to say things like "You'll be okay" or "When you finish this round of chemo, we'll go to Sea World" or "We'll pray hard and God will get us through." They don't turn it into a melodrama about themselves.

"You should have listened more. Stayed on track—"

"So *I've* caused this? By going part-time?"

"You didn't need to. You're smarter than that . . . that certificate in beauty—"

"You don't know anything. It's a diploma—"

"It's a joke."

"Stay out of my life."

"And that boy—"

"Fuck off." She says it so loud, the whole ward must hear it. "You're jealous."

I don't know how the girl can fight back, but she does, again and again.

The ward manager asks the mother to leave and I see her take off, her hair drawn back in that tortoiseshell claw, a hand swiping at tears.

But the fight's not yet over. I hear the new girl lay into Nina.

"Go away."

"I need to hook up the new bags," Nina's saying. "Yours are empty."

"No!" the girl yells, with more energy than I could muster. "No *more*. Leave me *alone!*"

There's a flurry of nurses in the corridor and, soon, Patrick's shoes as he walks to Room 2 and closes the door behind him. I imagine him standing there, hands clasped, asking delicately about her "feelings." She fights him, too.

It doesn't end until later, with Dr. Aneta and probably something like Valium. "Fine, give it to me," the new girl says. "Give me the lot."

Now there's a silence that seeps through our wall. Six centimeters isn't so solid after all.

There's so much she doesn't understand yet: that it gets better, that it's not the doctors' fault. *Don't struggle*, I want to say. *Don't pull the emergency exit lever. Take the pills and, for what it's worth, enjoy the ride.*

I wish I could tell her this.

I wish I could tell her how lucky she is.

• • •

Returning to bed after my third piss of the night, I see a star on the floor. It's as if it found its own way there, skimming under the door and across the smooth linoleum.

There's still a bit of glow left in it. I pick it up and let it lead me back to bed.

When I'd told the girl about the star on her ceiling, I hadn't wanted her to return it. Why does she keep getting my messages wrong?

I hope I haven't made her sadder.

I hear her toilet flush. Three a.m.

I wonder how it feels to lie in a room this size without anyone to share it with.

I don't reach for the iPad tonight. I'm not in the mood for

updates on the winners and losers. Instead, I keep hold of the star as it fades. I watch until it disappears completely, and even then I feel its shape in my palm.

Head to head, we lie.

At least, I think, she's not fighting me.

5
Zac

Around lunchtime, I convince Mum I'm desperate for a spearmint milkshake from the cafeteria—a guaranteed way to get her out of my room. I need to knock on the wall and tell the girl to take back the star. She wasn't supposed to return it to me.

I knock, but a man's voice answers. The girl's already gone.

Cam and I met in the common room way back in April. He was in for radiation and our cycles overlapped, so we'd play long games of pool, though I think he took it easy on me. Fresh from surgery, the scar on his head was a raised, violent C. C for Cam. *In case you forget.* It could have been C for the other word, the one that can't be named. Cam's tumor had been the size of a golf ball, and he carried one in his pocket for illustrative purposes. He'd thought his headaches were caused by getting dumped surfing too many times.

"I've . . . what do you call it?" he calls through the wall. "Relapsed. Like you did."

It's not fair that the two words should be so close: *relapse, remission.* They should be at opposite ends of the dictionary.

His hair's grown back curly, he says. "But now the bastard's back and I've got to get zapped again." He's an electrician, he reminds me, so he can handle it. He boasts he's been surfing every day since finishing treatment the first time. Last week he scoffed at a two-meter tiger shark. "What could it do to me?" He laughs through the wall. I can almost hear the sea in his voice.

Nina's lured into his room more often than mine. There's not much of an age difference between them, I reckon. I over-hear their small talk and the buzz in her voice. When she comes into my room, a grin still plays at her lips, a different shape than the one she usually gives me. Her cheeks are the color of her ladybug clip. I watch her change my IV fluids and reset the monitor, wondering how she can let herself be sucked in when she knows what I do: that his twenty-five percent chance has slid to ten. Even ten percent is generous.

Fuck, I don't want to do this. I don't want to think about numbers, but that's what happens here.

In school, chance was straightforward:

> *If a die is rolled, what is the probability of rolling*
>   *a 3?*
> 1:6
> *If two dice are rolled, what is the probability of*
>   *rolling two 3s?*
> 1:36

I liked math. I liked that I knew where I stood. But now?

If a 32-year-old man has a brain tumor removed,
  then after eight months the cancer comes back,
  what are the chances for survival?
1:11
Convert this to a percentage.
9.09%

Math is inescapable here. Doctors rattle off ratios of white blood cells and leukocytes. Nurses measure my temperature and weight, calculating milligrams of methotrexate, prednisone, cyclophosphamide. They chart my progress, praising my improvement in increments, as if I'm somehow responsible for the upward gradient. More than the oldies' with dodgy bowels, mine is a graph worthy of excitement and optimism. I am their star student.

Unlike Cam. Fucking Google. On some websites his chances are pegged as 1:10; on others, 1:14. When he bangs on my wall and says, "Zac-boy, turn to channel four. It's *The Goodies*! Goodie goodie, yum yum," I wonder if he looks at the same sites I do.

I know to keep these stats to myself, away from Mum and Patrick and Facebook and whoever else would worry. I have to file them away and focus on what's in front of me: Nina.

"Cam wants to give you a lesson when you're out," she says, washing her hands.

"In math?"

"In surfing, doofus."

"Me?" The human Rice Krispy? At least I'll float.

"Cam says he'll take you surfing after Christmas. He's got

a nine-foot longboard that would be perfect for you. He asked for your cell number."

I'll be shark bait for sure. Still, I tear out a page and write down my number. That man walks around with a giant C on his head, and now spots in his lungs, and still he dares the ocean. I can't say no to him. I add

> Or Facebook me: Zac Meier (second one listed, you might not recognize me!)

Mum delivers my note to Cam then stays in to chat. Without a significant other — his dog and roommate don't count — Cam finds a surrogate in my mum, who brings teas and biscuits. In the real world they would have nothing in common — Mum's a farmer from down south; Cam's a surfing electrician with a Ford pickup — but here on the ward, the usual rules don't seem to matter as much.

Nina eases a thermometer into my ear. Today's hair clip is a reindeer.

"This end of the ward is better, don't you reckon?" I'm as casual as I can be with a thermometer sticking out of my head.

"Yeah?"

"It's brighter, or something. Better feng shui. Good for patients of a . . . younger age. Like Cam. And even . . . *younger* than that."

"Really?"

"It would make sense, I reckon," pushing on, "for the young ones — like Cam, or . . . whoever — to be put up in this end . . . in the future. You know, whenever the next hypothetical young one has to come back in."

"As hypothetically young as Mia, you mean?" Nina flicks her wrist and records numbers in my file.

Mia. The name suits her. "Is she okay?"

Nina snaps the pen onto the clipboard. Whatever the reality, I know she won't bullshit me.

"She'll be fine, Zac. Don't you worry about her."

But I know this already. I've Googled it.

That girl's got the best odds of all of us.

• • •

Two days later, Patrick comes in saying he has good news.

"I'm cured?"

"Um . . . well, no. I mean, you will be, Zac, in five years . . . officially . . ."

"You've got me a date with Emma Watson?"

His face cracks with relief. "Maybe. I mean, I haven't read the fine print. We're nominating you for a Make-A-Wish award."

I've heard about these wishes, granted to under-eighteens with life-threatening illnesses. I've seen photos of kids in helicopter flights or at Disneyland hugging Mickey and Minnie Mouse. The thing is, they're prepubescent—the kids, that is, not the giant mice—and I'm having trouble picturing myself as the latest Make-A-Wish pinup guy.

"Why?"

"Because you're such a fighter, Zac."

"Like Muhammad Ali?"

"Well, maybe." Patrick sits sideways on the end of my bed and rubs at his corduroy trousers. "No, not really. It's because you never complain. You're always . . . on top of things." I can see what he's thinking: *Unlike that girl . . .*

"I get it. More like Hulk Hogan, then."

"Zac!" Mum points a licorice stick at me. She's lectured me about taking advantage of Patrick's goodwill. Like the other staff here, he's used to psychologizing about adult issues, such as bankruptcy and infertility and the unfairness of life and blah blah blah.

"Maybe more like a fighter at war," Patrick suggests.

"So this room is, like, Afghanistan, and my leukemia is the Taliban?"

"If you like . . ."

"A metaphor. Thanks. Can I use that in English?"

"Sure. Right, then," he says, standing. "Put some thought into what you want. Emma Watson, eh? Hermione from *Harry Potter*, you mean? Why not? We can all dream . . ."

"Be nice," Mum says, after Patrick's washed his hands and waved himself out.

"*You* be nice or I'll wish a Jenny Craig membership on you."

The truth is, I don't want to go to Disneyland or drive a Formula 1 with Michael Schumacher. When I finally get out of this room, the last thing I want is a fuss being made over me. All I want is to get under that huge blue sky, mucking about on the farm with Dad and Evan and playing football with the guys. Even helping Bec with the animals. I just want to be outside again, like I'm supposed to be.

Besides, I don't deserve an award. I'm not a fighter and I'm probably not very brave. I haven't saved a kid from drowning, or sailed around the world. Playing three hours of Xbox a day doesn't make me a hero. I've lain on my bed for twenty-seven consecutive days and successfully mastered my bowel movements. I've succeeded in losing 100 percent of the hair on my head, which has somehow managed to double in size. And, after seventeen days with new marrow, I've finally begun to make some white blood cells of my own, so the tests show. None of this is groundbreaking stuff.

I've watched documentaries about prisoners of war who survived for years by chewing charcoal dust and putting maggots onto wounds to eat their infections. Now *that* deserves a trip to Disneyland. In here I have a fridge-freezer, television and Xbox, air conditioning at a constant 70 degrees, hot meals and three snacks delivered daily, and someone who makes my bed.

I don't moan about my treatment because what's the point? The way I figure it, this is just a blip. The average life span for an Australian male is currently seventy-nine years, or 948 months. This hospital stay, plus the first rounds of chemo and the follow-up visits, add up to about nine months. That's only 1.05 percent of my life spent with needles and chemicals, which, put into perspective, is less than one of the tiles out of the eighty-four on the ceiling.

So in the scheme of things, it's nothing. And it's definitely not worthy of a Make-A-Wish award. If anyone deserves a prize it's Cam, but at thirty-two, he's too old.

Nina deserves an award too. She knows the odds and still lets herself fall for him.

"So, why Emma Watson?" Mum says later. Even Mum's braver than me. She *chooses* to endure this.

I'm the least brave of everyone. I never signed up for this war. Leukemia conscripted me, the fucker.

6

Zac

Facebook tells me I have two new friend requests. With 679 friends, I really don't need any more. Before I got sick, my tally was in the mid-400s, and even that was a stretch: school friends, ex–school friends, and guys from the football and cricket teams. But now I have "friends" from everywhere: distant relatives, patients and their families from the hospital, and members of various teen cancer networks I was coerced to join, who clutter my profile page with jokes, borderline-spiritual quotes, and acronyms I can't always translate.

"Online communication is essential," Patrick told me, "to survive the isolation of your Isolation." But I have a feeling my "friends" benefit more than I do.

The most entertaining thing about Facebook has been rejecting Mum's persistent friend requests.

"You're with me every hour of the day, Mum. Why do we need to Facebook each other too?"

"I just want to see what you're up to."

"You do see what I'm up to. You see everything. In real time."

"But I only have fourteen friends," she says, as if pity could break me.

"Then you need to get out more. Go talk to real friends, or visit Aunty Trish. She only lives three suburbs away. Or better still, go *home*."

"I'll go when you go, in seven days," she reminds me, as if I've managed to forget. As if.

I reject Mum's friend request again, then open the second one.

I'd expected it to be from Cam.

Friend request: Mia Phillips

0 mutual friends

It's a name I don't recognize, with a face I think I've seen. I stare into the photo to be sure. She has a low-cut cami and a necklace with half a silver heart. Her arms are draped around the shoulders of other girls. Is it her?

I look up at my round window. She's not there, of course. There's just the white wall and two-thirds of the hygiene sign, now framed with festive red and green tinsel. But it's the newbie's face on the screen; it has to be. The girl with the tap to my knock.

She's asking me to be her friend and it's caught me mid-breath, mid-moan, mid-everything.

My finger hovers over "Confirm," but I'm confused. How does she know who I am?

"Mum? Has Cam gone home?"

"No. They shifted him to Room Six."

"When?"

"While you were sleeping."

I lower my volume and my voice falls an octave. "Then who's in Room Two?"

Mum shrugs as if it's none of her business all of a sudden, then offers me a marshmallow. She knows exactly who's in Room 2.

The screen gives me two options:

Confirm   Not Now

"She wasn't due back till Tuesday. Isn't that what Nina said?" I thought she was on a cycle of five days on and five days off.

"I can't remember. What's a seven-letter word for 'moccasin'?"

I don't need another Facebook friend, especially one who burns me crap CDs and peels off glow-in-the-dark stars for no reason. A girl who gets my messages all wrong. Who's so full of fight.

But she's alone, after all . . .

My finger overrides my brain and presses the screen.

Confirm

I brace myself but there are no seismic shifts or deafening alarms. This hasn't changed anything. She's just become one more fake friend on my profile page.

Then, *tap*.

Was it the cleaner next door? Or a girl's knuckle?

Tap.

I catch Mum glaring at the wall.

"Was that you?" she asks, and I shake my head.

"Maybe there's a mouse."

Tap, the wall insists. *Tap tap*.

Holy crap! In the space of two hours, the new girl's moved in next door, Facebook-friended me, *and* tapped me? This is happening at warp speed.

I scramble to her page to see her life exposed in comments and photos and emoticons.

Beach this w'end Mia. You in?

Why werent you at Georgies? Best. night. EVER!

I see her latest update, posted three weeks ago:

So over this dumbass ankle

The comments that follow are way off target:

Too much dancing!!!?

Didn't you get antibiotics or something?

Mamma mia u unco spaz ;)

I skim down the page, looking for more.

I see older updates about shoes and dresses for the school dance a month ago. There's a photo of splayed hands with ten different shades of nail polish, followed by trails of inane comments by some of her 1,152 friends. Seriously? Who knows that many people?

But there's no "c" word. There's not even a *chemo*.

The beach? It doesn't make sense. Has she really fooled them into believing it's just a sore leg? The new girl might have good odds, but it's still cancer, and it sucks. It'll suck for ages.

Tap.

Her friends have been posting crap about summer holidays and pre-Christmas sales, not realizing Mia's been in and out of the hospital, feeling like death. Why hasn't she told them?

I scroll further and see her life in reverse, back through a couple of whines about a sore ankle, then back to before, to the usual complaints about school, to invitations to the beach, to Karrinyup, to her photos tagged at the Big Day Out and Summadayze. I see her Facebook life exposed in a beautiful, colorful rush, but I still see none of her.

Then my iPad makes an unexpected *blop* sound and in the bottom right corner of the screen, the chat box tells me, *Mia is typing . . .*

Blop.

Mia: Is that YOU?

Shit! Can she sense I'm on her page? Does she think I'm spying? But *she* invited *me!*

Five minutes ago I was watching a cricket match against Sri Lanka, and now I'm being belted with stressful taps and questions from the girl next door. Mia. I need to slow her down, or speed myself up. And why is *YOU* in capitals?

Tap.

"Zac?" Mum's voice is testy. "Was that you?"

What the hell? Which do I answer first? The wall or the Facebook question? Or my mum? And what do I say, anyway?

Another *blop.*

Mia: Hey!
R U there? Zac Meier?

The cursor flashes angrily beneath the question, but I'm a rabbit in her headlights.

Tap!

There was definite knuckle-crunching in that one. Her demands are in stereo.

Shit. I type:

Zac: I'm her

But my fingers slip across the iPad's touch screen and I press "Enter" prematurely. There's a pause long enough to regret my error. Long enough for confusion to sink in next door.

Mia: R u a girl?
Zac: No

I opt for a short message. Brief is better. This touch screen is a minefield.

Zac: I'm here
A male

I add that last part for clarification, though I lose a few seconds considering the options of "boy" and "man." Surely she knows I'm male! She's seen me through my window at least four times. Could it be that my constant proximity to females—my mother, the predominantly female staff, possibly even my bone marrow—has seriously compromised my Y chromosomes? More questions are fired:

Mia: Who r u?
Is that u next door?
Zac: Yes. Rm 1. Yr neighbor. Zac
Male

I say it again for emphasis.

Mia: But yr profile pic is a girl . . .

Shit. She's right. I'd forgotten about the German Beerfest girl with long blond braids and generous cleavage.

Zac: not me. thats a joke

How do I explain in abbreviation about the nickname Helga and the unknown German donor?

> **Zac:** Long story . . . am part Helga . . . possibly . . .
> **Mia:** ?
> **Zac:** !

What else can I say?

The cursor blinks at me in disbelief. I need to prove I'm me, so I reach across and knock on the wall. It sounds different from before.

Mum is watching me. She eyes my fist. I'd forgotten she was here.

> **Mia:** y did u put yr number in my drawer?
> **Zac:** Not yours. Cam's. Misbake

Why does this have to be so hard? Cam must have left my note behind accidentally. So much for the cleaners.

> **Zac:** Mistake. Mistake!!!!

The repetition and exclamation marks look pissed off, as if I emphatically regret friending her, which I do, but only because I'm making a complete dick of myself.

She types nothing, and I think she regrets it too. Why bother being friends with someone you can't meet? Someone who looks the way I do and types so recklessly.

I take a deep breath and start again. I need to spell this out.

> **Zac:** Didnt put note in yr room.
> Am stuck in here.
> Note for someone else — Cam. He's in room 6 now.
> But mistake ok.
> Ok?

She answers my question with another.

> **Mia:** y stuck?

The cursor blinks curiously. How do I type this? My weakness through last year, thinking it was too much football. The bruises and fatigue and flu. Then the tests and diagnosis and those six months of chemo, then life — life! — then relapse, followed by the search for a bone marrow transplant donor and the total body irradiation, then the quarantine for the German marrow to take hold as I rebuild my immune system so my leukocytes will be ready for the world. But until then I'm stuck here, stuck here to graft and build and heal and wait and get excited about the smallest things, like a tap on the wall and someone, finally, my own age to talk to.

> **Zac:** Just stuck. 7 more days. Not so bad . . . :-/

I'm left looking at the blank space for ages. Did I say too much? Did it sound like I was asking for pity?

I sense her slipping away, her eyes glazing over, wanting to return to her Facebook page of healthy, popular friends from the real world, with tans, oversize sunglasses, and heart-shaped pendants. They could be models in magazines. I want to tell her

I'm one of those people too—well, kind of—even if I do currently resemble a Rice Krispy. But all I say is

> **Zac:** U can play yr music if you want. I hate gaga but
> **Mia:** Me too
> **Zac:** ?
> **Mia:** it was a gift.
>   & good mum-repellant
> **Zac:** ?
> **Mia:** guaranteed
> **Zac:** didn't work on mine
>   u can play anything u want. Its yr room.

There's no response so I go stupidly on.

> **Zac:** Take it easy. dont be sa

This iPad should have an override button to stop me screwing up.

> **Zac:** d

I add this last letter, but I don't know why I type this either, as if I'm the Sad Police. I'm not. She can be whatever she wants to be.

Apparently what she wants to be is alone. Her green chat symbol disappears and I'm left feeling like I've said all the wrong things, spelled all the wrong ways.

Don't be sad? Why isn't there a significant other—like her mum, or the guy in the hat who'd visited that day—to spew out dumb stuff instead of me? She needs someone beside her to tell her that everything is going to be all right, that it's not for long; that at seventeen, she has sixty-seven years of life ahead of her, according to current statistics, and this is just a blip, a time-out from her real life, less than one square on her ceiling.

I hear her body rising from the bed next door and, soon, the toilet flush. If she's throwing up, I hope it's because of the Cisplatin and not because of me.

I linger on her Facebook page long enough to learn she'll be going into year twelve next year; that she's been training for a Diploma of Beauty Therapy one day a week. That she loves Tim Burton films, Ryan Reynolds, Flume, and Peanut M&M's. That she hates bananas. And she's in a relationship, it says, with Rhys Granger.

I switch the iPad off. We might be "friends," but we're not friends, and apart from the obvious, we have little in common. It would feel weird to stalk her wall any longer.

"A six-letter word meaning 'ostracize'?" Mum asks.

But words fail me.

7
Zac

Status: **5 days to go. Dying of boredom. Suggestions?**

Mum's assigned herself a project: teaching herself to knit from a *Knitting for Dummies* book. At forty-nine, and a soon-to-be-grandmother, she decided it was time. Her first attempt is a scarf for Bec's yet-to-be-born baby. She clicks and clacks using wool from a packet that was hygienically sealed to prevent germs from entering our cocoon. Cast thirty-eight, knit-stitch eight, purl twenty-four. It sounds like aerobics. Mum could do with some aerobics.

I need a project too. Something to make my last week skip along like her stitching, quickening with increasing confidence. Instead, time feels like a lump of clay in my useless, puffy hands. Five big fat days to go.

It's not that Mum hasn't offered to teach me—she bought spare knitting needles in the hope we would purl in sync— but I threatened to use one to stab myself in the eye. I'd rather watch repeats of *Glee* than take up knitting. Besides, I need to pay more attention to my image.

"I need a hat," I tell her.

"I'll have to finish the scarf first." Since when do babies wear scarves, anyway?

"Not knitted. Bought. A cap, or something, like Ryan Reynolds would wear. Can you get me a hat?"

"Why would you need a hat inside?"

"It's not for sun protection. It's more for . . . ego protection. My head is too pale."

Mum glances up mid-row. "Who's Ryan Reynolds? And what's wrong with your head?"

"I'm a human light bulb. I want a hat. A cool hat. A manly hat. A hat hat."

"All right, Dr. Seuss."

"But not from the hospital store. Somewhere . . . cooler. Could you do that?"

"What, right now? After thirty days, you've decided you need a hat right now?"

"Pretty much."

Mum exaggerates a sigh as she finishes the row, and then she places the needles and wool in her lap. "You're a funny one. Is this about the scarf? Because I'm doing one for the baby first?"

"Can't a man have a hat?"

"Do you need to talk to Patrick?"

"I *need* . . ." I repeat, exasperated, "a hat. And a mother who doesn't ask so many questions."

"Tetchy," she mutters, tossing her handbag over a shoulder. "I'll get some ice cream while I'm out, then. So, draw me a picture of this manly hat."

I tear a page from the neglected diary and draw something similar—but not too similar—to the hat Mia's boyfriend was wearing when he came in a week ago.

He's wearing it again today as he passes my round window, crossing paths with Mum in the corridor. I wonder if she takes any notice of this guy, with his fixed expression and fistful of carnations.

The conversation next door is too quiet to hear. Mia's speaking, at least, which is more than she's done for the past two days. I've wanted to tell her that it gets better; that this will pass. I hope Rhys is saying these things to her now. I hope he's being the significant other that her mother couldn't be.

There are already twenty-four comments on my latest post asking for a project. There are predictable suggestions from people I barely know—make a scrapbook of your journey; write a letter to yourself in one year's time; monogram a Christmas stocking—to ideas from mates and my brother: build an Eiffel Tower out of used needles (Alex); sell your old marrow on eBay (Matt); convince the nurses to star in a porn movie (Evan). The least-offensive suggestion comes from Rick, another Emma Watson fan: back-to-back Harry Potter movies. Easy.

Mia hasn't commented, not that I'd expected her to. I refresh her page again and again, waiting for her to add something about the hospital, her dumbass ankle, or even the creepy Helga-boy from next door. But her page remains unnaturally cheerful and my eyes ache from watching it. Her status update, posted last night, says:

Still chilling down south. Anyone got tix to Future Music Fest?

I read her friends' banter about the lineup. None of them asks about her ankle.

Don't they realize how wrong they are about her life? How sick and sad Mia is? I'll bet the only one who knows is in with her now, and he doesn't stay long. I hear the door open and close, and then I see Rhys in the corridor, empty-handed. A minute later I spot him through my rectangular window as he emerges from the main entrance, seven stories down. He lets himself into a car in the five-minute parking bay. Then he zooms off, leaving behind the hospital and its sickness and the seventeen-year-old girl who's crying softly in the next room.

It's more painful than any pop song.

If I could get up and go in there, I would. At least, I think I would.

I'd go in there and sit on her bed. I'd rub her back. I'd put my arm around her, I think, if that's what she wanted, the way Mum used to do with me.

But I'm stuck in this room, burdened with the sad sounds that no one else can hear.

• • •

When Mum returns from shopping, she presents me with a tea cozy with earflaps.

"What the hell?"

"The man at the store said it's on trend. He said Burt Reynolds would wear it."

"Who?"

She rolls her eyes. "The actor. You know, *Smoky and the Bandit.*"

Is she for real?

"It was your idea," she says.

I'm tempted to throw up in it, but Mum pushes it over my head. She steps back and looks at me like I'm a work of graffiti she's trying to decipher.

"Didn't a gay cowboy wear one in that mountain movie?"

"Not exactly the look I was after, Mum."

"Well, you need to work on your drawing skills." She crumples my hat sketch and chucks it into the bin. "Why don't you? I could get some fruit in here . . . make a still life out of it. Get you a *Drawing for Dummies* book."

Mum's testing my patience more than ever. It wasn't so bad with chemo: we could handle five days together, knowing that back at home we'd have five days of our own space. But a month together is cabin fever territory. Hysteria is just a sideways glance away.

"You know that newbie?" I say, hoping to kill two birds with one stone.

"I don't think she's that new anymore." Mum gets me on a technicality.

"The girl formerly known as newbie. Mia."

"Mia?"

"She's next door. Can you go say hi? Take Scrabble with you."

Mum sniffs at the idea.

"At least the word puzzle," I say.

"She doesn't seem the . . . word puzzle type."

Friendly, she means. The tea-loving, scone-eating, happy-go-lucky sort, like most of the patients and their significant others. *The girl's grumpy,* she means, adolescent and angry, the way Bec used to be as a teenager.

"Maybe tomorrow," Mum says. "You know, I think that hat suits you."

"Pass me a knitting needle."

Instead, Mum hands me a bowl of cookie dough ice cream. I eat it, even though it tastes sweeter than it should. It's something to do, at least.

I listen to my new albums with my earbuds in, choosing which songs I'd burn for Mia if I had the guts to.

Five days to go.

· · ·

I leave the toilet unflushed and tiptoe back to bed.

I switch on the iPad and scroll through blogs of patients from around the world. It always amazes me how people confess their fears to a global, unseen audience. How they upload hairless photos of themselves or painful poems in rhyming couplets. Or make promises to gods of one religion or another. Are they brave or just bored? I even read their prayers. It makes me feel less alone, at three a.m., to know I'm not the only one shut in.

I track the progress of the hopeful and hopeless, the winners and losers. And each time I read about someone's death to leukemia, there's a grim sense of relief. I could never admit this to anyone—and I feel like an absolute bastard—but their loss helps me believe, in some cosmic way, that my chances of survival are boosted. Someone else has chalked a hit on the scoreboard. It means I'm safer, doesn't it?

I don't know these people and I don't want them to die, but they make my odds look better. I have to believe in the math. Mum is snoring beside me for the thirty-second night in a row, and even though she can irritate the hell out of me, I can't let her down. She needs me to beat this.

I read the blogs of parents with children too young to type for themselves. I read panicked letters on forums from people who found out too late and don't even get the chance of chemo or a transplant. Again I feel lucky. Then I feel guilty.

Then I see her at the bottom of my screen. She's nothing but a small green dot peering up at me: a glow-in-the-dark planet. As if she's been watching.

I'm not the only one not sleeping.

The green dot means go. Should I go? She's been so quiet these past two days.

But she writes first.

> **Mia:** Helga?
> **Zac:** it's zac
> **Mia:** U awake?
> **Zac:** What do you reckon?
> **Mia:** True.
> I cant sleep.
> **Zac:** Its the 3 am curse.
> **Mia:** curse? What drugs u on?
> **Zac:** just isolation. Enough to make you crazy
> **Mia:** Helga I feel like shit.
> **Zac:** Ur supposed to. Chemo does that.
> It's Zac . . . by the way
> It gets better

I add. And then:

> **Zac:** You'll get better.

I hope it doesn't look like an empty promise.

> **Mia:** sure
> **Zac:** for sure
> **Mia:** Will u?

Like a dart, her question finds me. She has good aim.

> **Zac:** I'm nearly better. Brand new Helga marrow.
> **Mia:** u looked really sick

My head sinks heavier into my pillow. She's right. At least she's honest enough to say so.

> **Zac:** Chemo. steroids. Lack of sun.
> **Mia:** So u wont die?

The "d" word jumps off the screen. Everyone else here avoids it.

> **Zac:** No
> **Mia:** Good.

What do I type in response? *Thanks*?

> **Zac:** New marrow's grafted now.
>   We're all getting better.

Mia: What happens to someones facebook when they die?

Zac: I don't know . . .

Mia: Where do the profiles of dead people go?

Zac: U'll have to ask Zuckerberg.

Mia: Who?

Zac: The god of facebook.

Mia: Where do their other things go?

Like mobile phones and all the music on ipods?

I imagine mountains of phones. Songs forgotten in clouds.

Zac: Why?

Mia: FUCKING BORED. How can u STAND this place?

Zac: don't have a choice. Sleep helps. Seinfeld.

Modern Family.

Mia: They put a tube down my nose and it killed.

Zac: ur not eating?

Mia: everything tastes smoky.

chocolate tastes like wax :(

Zac: Try grilled cheese sandwiches with ketchup. A chemo classic.

Let the cheese cool first though

Mia: aren't u bored?

Zac: out of my brain. 30 days in the same room.

Mia: ?!!!

Zac: Been stuck in this room since November 18.

Nearly done though. U too. 2 cycles down.

Mia: 3 to go :-(

Zac: only 5?? Ur lucky.

Mia: Lucky????

Zac: So lucky. Dont u know?

She must know, mustn't she? That females her age with osteosarcoma have an eighty percent survival rate, but hers is above ninety because of the location. If all the cancer gets zapped and the tumor's cut out, it'll be over ninety-five. Doesn't she realize how good ninety-five percent is?

Instead, I type:

> **Zac:** Ur the luckiest on the ward
> **Mia:** Lucky = winning the lotto
> **Zac:** U should buy a lotto ticket then
> **Mia:** Ur a funny guy
> **Zac:** so everyone keeps saying
> **Mia:** Not funny ha ha, but funny hmmm . . . :-*
> Ok sleepy. Thanks.
> **Zac:** Anytime.
> **Mia:** See ya Helga.
> **Zac:** Zac!

There's a soft tap at the wall that could be accidental.

I switch off the iPad and the room fades to black, but there's no chance of sleep. Our conversation loops in my head like a song on repeat. It's not a perfect song, but it's an improvement on the Lady Gaga kind.

Mia's funny, in a *ha ha* kind of way.

I lie in bed thinking of all I typed, and the things I'll type tomorrow at three a.m., the hour when rules are suspended.

8

Zac

I'm so hot right now.

Over 103.1 degrees. So much for my perfect graph.

The cleaners threw out everything of Mum's: tubs of ice cream, reading glasses, and crosswords. Even the calendar's in a hazard bag in an industrial bin somewhere. My room's been emptied, scrubbed, and sterilized.

Mum's gone too. Dr. Aneta ordered her to take her cold of unspecified origin back home with her. Dad phoned to say he was coming up, but I talked him out of it. The room's too small for him. Bec offered, but I'd hate for her to pick up bugs in her pregnancy. Besides, what would be the point? It's not like I can entertain anyone.

My platelets have plummeted to 12, leukocytes to 0.4, and hemoglobin to 8. My total white blood count has nose-dived to 0.8 and I'm too sick to give a shit. I'm slumped in the pink chair while Veronica makes my bed. My sheets are soaked with last night's sweat. Again.

It's just a cold. A stupid freaking cold that I'm too pathetic to fight on my own. The line from my Broviac leads to two bags of antibiotics. I use the urine bottles. Cleaners ferry them away.

I keep the blinds drawn, not knowing day from night. It's all the same. Psychedelic dreams weave through sleeping and waking, looping around themselves. I only had four days to go. How long ago was that?

I'd forgotten this blanket of fatigue and how it holds you down. I'd forgotten the sweats and shivers and endlessness. Nurses offer to play Call of Duty, but I can't manage it. I'm not interested in TV or the Internet.

This is a good thing, Nina insists, keeping a hand on my shoulder. "It's better your white blood cells get a thumping in here than out there."

Come on, Helga. Show some spine and fight back.

• • •

Later, when I can't be bothered to sleep, I drag the iPad toward me and switch it on. The brightness dazzles me. It's just past three a.m.

My Facebook profile has been stormed by well-wishers. *It's just a cold,* I want to inform everyone. *Don't stress.* But I don't have the energy.

Mia: Helga?

I see her name rise into chat. I hadn't realized she was there.

Zac: Zac

Mia: U ok?

I don't need to lie to her. It is what it is. She only wants the truth.

Zac: ordinary
Mia: U said ud be home by now.
Zac: Caught a cold. Beat the crap out of me.
Mia: :-(
Zac: drugs starting to kick in.
Hows yr 3rd round?
Mia: its my 4th

Shit. How long have I been sick?

Zac: u in Room 2?
Mia: yeah.
Zac: hi
Mia: hi. Happy fucking christmas.
Zac: Today?
Mia: 4 days ago.
Zac: Oh. Happy Christmas
Mia: I feel like shit
Zac: me too
Mia: like I'm sucking poison
Zac: it's normal.
Mia: yeah?
Zac: it'll pass. it all does.

I remind us both.

Mia: I don't want to die

The cursor blinks, waiting for me. Without my mum sleeping beside me, I don't have to rush this. No typos, no clichés.

> **Zac:** U won't
> **Mia:** I'm only 17
> **Zac:** U won't
> **Mia:** a woman died today
> **Zac:** Who?
> **Mia:** dunno. Room 9
> **Zac:** What cancer?
> **Mia:** dunno. She was old

I've never known anyone to die here. Death usually takes place in the comfort of a patient's home after the hospital has handed them over to family or palliative care or God, or whoever else will listen. They're supposed to sort out their wills and choose the songs for their funerals, say their goodbyes, and go out in their own beds surrounded by loved ones. It must have been unexpected.

> **Mia:** Lots of people were in there.
> **Zac:** you saw?
> **Mia:** through her window.
> The nurses stood in the hall.
> It must've been just after . . .
> She was skinny. ppl were
> crying.

I let her keep going. It's the most she's ever typed. I think I hear her fingers on her keyboard.

>**Mia:** have you ever seen a dead body?
>**Zac:** not a human. You? Before?
>**Mia:** My nan at her funeral.
>I laughed cos they used the wrong makeup.
>The lipstick was pink gloss and I kept thinking about how long it would stay on.
>Longer than her lips?
>How long would it take for pearl earrings to drop from her ears?
>**Zac:** you laughed?
>**Mia:** I was 8.

All the relatives I've known are still alive: four grandparents, two uncles, an aunt, a great-aunt, four cousins, one brother, and a sister. I've never even been to a real funeral.

>**Zac:** In kindergarten, a boy drowned in a dam.
>The teacher said he'd gone to a better place.
>I thought she meant McDonald's.
>**Mia:** :-)

I wonder what Mia looks like with a smile. Not a posed one, like in her Facebook photos, but a lazy real one, slumped against a pillow in the middle of the night.

>**Mia:** pick it up quick
>**Zac:** pick wh

The shrill sound punctures the silence, twice, three times, before I can knock the handset from the wall. I've never heard the internal phone—everyone else calls me on my cell. I hold the bulky receiver, forgetting what to do with it.

"Helga?"

I swallow. "Zac."

"Are you okay . . . to talk?"

"Yeah," I tell her, though my throat's thick and husky. "I'm okay."

"Do you believe in ghosts?"

How come she asks the kinds of things everyone else avoids? Is it because we're still, technically, strangers? Or because it's 3:33 a.m. and the normal rules don't apply? My breath whistles through the holes.

"Um . . . I don't know."

"Yes or no?"

"No."

"Heaven?"

"No."

"God?"

"No."

"No?"

"You do?"

When she pauses, I hear her breath whistling too. "Can I tell you something?"

"Yeah. Yes."

"When the woman died in Room Nine, there was something else . . . in the corridor."

"What?"

"Like something I couldn't see."

"A ghost?"

"I don't know. It felt like . . . like that old woman was standing next to me. Like she was watching too. It freaked me out."

I know all about death. I know that one person dies in Australia every three minutes and forty seconds. I know that tomorrow, 42 Australians will die because of smoking, almost four on roads, and almost six by suicide.

In this coming week, 846 will die from cancer: 156 will be from lung, 56 from breast, 30 from melanoma, 25 from brain tumors like Cam's. And 34 of them will have had leukemia, like me.

Google tells me everything I need to know about death except what comes after.

What can I say about a ghost in the corridor? How can I tell her it was her imagination and nothing more? When I was little I believed in Jesus and Santa, spontaneous combustion, and the Loch Ness monster. Now I believe in science, statistics, and antibiotics. But is that what a girl wants to hear at 3:40 a.m.?

"Helga?"

What I really want to say is how good it is to hear her voice. "I'm here."

"You think I'm crazy?"

"Depends. What drugs are you on?"

"Does it hurt to die?" she asks.

"No." This I believe.

"I haven't even lived yet."

"Yeah, you have, and you will. Until you're eighty-four, at least."

"But still," she says. "If I did, what a stupid way to die."

I take a lozenge from a packet and put it in my mouth. "Actually, there are plenty of stupider ways."

"Stupider than a lump on my ankle?"

"As stupid as watering a Christmas tree with the lights plugged in."

"Helga, no one has *ever* done that."

"Thirty-one people have been electrocuted that way. And that's just in Australia." I hear her laughing through the wall and it makes all my sickness disappear. "Did you know three Australians die every year testing batteries on their tongues?"

"No way."

"Yep. Then there's death by vending machine. For future reference, if a bag of chips ever gets stuck in one, just walk away . . ."

"Are you talking crap?"

"The crappest way to die is drowning in sewage."

"No *way*."

"Last year a New York man fell into a sewer vat."

"Shit."

"Yeah, vat deaths are pretty common. Six Indian workers died in a vat of tomato sauce."

"Six?"

"One fell in; the other five jumped in to rescue her."

"You are so making this up."

"Cross my heart. There have been deaths in vats of oil, paper pulp, beer—"

"I wouldn't mind falling into a vat of chocolate."

"That's been done. New Jersey, 2009. A twenty-nine-year-old man—"

"How do you know all this?"

"I've had a lot of time on my hands."

I hear her breathing while I wait for what's coming.

"Helga, if you had the choice —"

"A vat of Emma Watsons."

"You've thought about it?"

"Of course. You?"

"Since chocolate's taken . . . a vat of Jelly Bellies? You do realize there's only one Emma Watson."

"Then she'll do."

Mia laughs. "Good luck with that."

The IV monitor whirs beside me. I'd forgotten it was there. For the last five minutes there have been no machines or meds or leukemia. There's only been two people with a phone line between them. I'd wanted to make Mia feel better — I hadn't expected it would rub off on me.

"Mia, one in two people get cancer," I say. "We're just getting ours out of the way early."

"I would've preferred to wait till I'm old."

"Mia?"

"Yeah?"

"Use the mouthwash. It's foul but it beats ulcers."

"That's what the nurses said."

"And sucking on ice cubes helps too."

"Yeah?"

"Trust me."

I'd meant it as a throwaway comment but she falls quiet, as if chewing it over.

"Okay."

9
Zac

"How are you feeling?" Nina asks. It's my forty-fourth day in, so I'm told. "Are you coping without your mum?"

"I'm a big boy."

Nina smiles and hands me four pills, two throat lozenges, three vitamins, and lip balm. She takes a thermometer from her pocket and puts it in my ear. Distracted, she keeps it in too long, looking at a midpoint between the bed and the wall. She seems tired. In her hair, a small koala holds tight to its branch.

"One hundred?" I guess.

"Ninety-nine point five," she says. "Not bad. Do you feel all right?"

"Do you?"

"Me?"

"You look like shit, Nina."

"Charmer. You must be better." She writes down my temperature and gives me an unconvincing smile. "Looking forward to the new year?"

"It's got to be better than this one."

"True. Keep your chin up, Zac."

"I am," I say, though it's *her* chin that needs lifting.

She moves her hands slowly as she washes them, then leaves. Without Mum around, I have no idea what's happening in the rest of the ward. Even Mia's gone quiet. I remain logged in, but she stays offline.

On her Facebook page, posts invite her to New Year's Eve parties. They've still got no clue she's next door, hooked up to chemo and hydration. Mia must believe she can keep the two worlds separate. That if she keeps her cancer to herself, it doesn't exist.

At midnight, fireworks flare at my window, their golds and pinks zipping and whistling. I hear the blaring of distant horns. Down the ward, explosions of party poppers are accompanied by shrieks.

I write to Mia.

Happy New Year!

But she doesn't respond. The new year rolls quietly, darkly in.

• • •

Status: Cold 0, Zac 1. FYI: platelets 48 and leukocytes 1000.
        That's a good thing. Happy NY! Outta here maybe Saturday.

I even ask Nina to take a photo of me, and I pose with two thumbs up. My face has deflated. I look new: rebuilt from the marrow out. I make this photo my new profile pic, replacing Helga, and the compliments start flooding in.

I commit myself to the Harry Potter endurance test. Eight films back to back is the kind of challenge I can handle.

I become obsessed with two things: the devolution of Daniel Radcliffe's acting abilities, and the evolution of Emma Watson's awesomeness. After she hits puberty, around about *The Prisoner of Azkaban*, there's an exponential increase in hotness. By the end of *The Deathly Hallows*, she's smokin'.

It must work some kind of magic, because after two days I'm itching for freedom. Doctors praise my progress, plotted on my chart in a staircase of ticks. I feel like new, thanks to Helga, and in part thanks to Emma Watson. If I walked out of this room right now and strode down the street with this hat on, people wouldn't stare. I'd be just another guy with a hat. Admittedly, an out-of-breath guy with skin like a vampire's. But girls like that, apparently.

"What's got into you?" Kate laughs when the PT session ends and I ask for more weights.

I like the burn in my muscles. I like my lungs sucking in oxygen. I like the air rushing up from the exercise bike, blowing at my face.

And I like standing on my feet by the window to look down on the outside world with its taxis and ambulances and smoking surgeons and visitors carrying helium balloons. Soon I'll be in that germ-filled air and I can't wait. This room is too small for me.

A postcard from Cam says he's doing great, working three days a week. He says he's got his longboard ready for me.

Bec sends me one of the new The Good Olive! Olive Oil and Petting Farm postcards. She tells me there've been four new kids and one alpaca born, and that according to her latest ultrasound, her own baby's the size of a mango.

My blood test results make the doctors beam. I am on top of this. Nina is beside herself.

But Mia says nothing. Her Facebook profile remains slick and lipsticked, as always. Her friends upload photos of vacations and New Year's parties, already discussing plans for their Valentine's Day formal in six weeks' time. They're still treating Mia like she's one of them.

Only I know better. I hear her in the night. Sometimes she throws up. Sometimes she cries. Sometimes she does both, one after the other.

She hasn't been online in three days, but I write her a message anyway.

> Hey neighbor,
>
> Did you try a grilled cheese sandwich? I have many more cooking tips where that came from . . .
>
> I read that a Spanish guy died yesterday in a vat of glue. Pretty tacky, huh? Thought you'd want to know ;-)
>
> I'll be leaving on Saturday so don't go knocking on the wall, unless you want to make friends with an oldie.
>
> Good luck with year 12. At least you'll only have to do it once! Your neighbor
> Zac.

Mia's green dot explodes into chat.

> **Mia:** Helga!
> **Zac:** long time no
> **Mia:** theres hair everywhere. Heaps. Over the pillow
> **Zac:** it's normal
> **Mia:** no, its NOT normal! Fucking everywhere

I'm surprised it lasted so long. I look again at her profile pic: the oversize sunglasses, the pose, the cami top, the thick brown hair. I think of my own hair: two millimeters of soft down.

> **Zac:** It'll grow back.
> **Mia:** my formal's in 6 weeks!!
> **Zac:** on the plus side there's one less thing to worry about.
> **Mia:** ?!
> **Zac:** Just sayin.
> **Mia:** U think it's funny my hair's falling out?!
> **Zac:** hmmm, no . . . but there are some cute wigs;-)
> **Mia:** FUCK U

It's a punch in the gut I don't need. My fingers flinch from the keyboard.

> **Mia:** R u teasing me?

I hadn't meant to. Most people lose their hair. She should've expected that.

Mia: U think this is FUNNY?!

Her typing is quick—quicker than mine. Quick like jabs. Of course it's not funny, but what else can you do? If you can't laugh at yourself, there's no point to any of this.

Mia: U THINK I WANT TO LOOK LIKE THIS?
Zac: I think u don't have a choice
Mia: U THINK I WANT TO GO BALD AND UGLY? LIKE U?

What the hell?

Mia: DONT LAUGH AT ME!
Zac: Im not
Mia: DONT FU

I go offline, my green dot dissolving to safety.

There's a thump at our wall and I don't know if she's swearing or apologizing. I don't answer—I'm not her punching bag. *Bang,* it goes again, and it jars right through me.

A message appears in my email, uninvited.

Ive already lost my holidays, xmas and new year to fucking
    cancer. It can't tke the only good thing left
I'm NOT wearing a fucking WIG to my FORMAL!!! Helga!
Helga?
I can't do this anymore
Helga

Neither can I. I switch off the iPad and tunnel under my blanket.

I hear her spew in her toilet and I don't care. I don't have the strength for the both of us.

• • •

At my rectangular window, I watch the patterns that people make below. Some stream in toward the entrance, carrying armfuls of flowers. Others scurry empty-handed back out to the street, feeding coins into the parking machine before scattering to the corners of the lot and driving to places far away.

Mia's mother moves in circles, pausing at the concrete-edged garden to inhale cigarettes. She looks too young to be the mother of a teenager. She seems too anxious, as if she could take flight at any moment.

To be honest, I miss mine. She knows how to be grounded when she needs to be, to make me do word puzzles even when I don't feel like it.

Mia's mother takes a last drag and darts for the entrance below. A minute later she's flitting past my door.

A swarm of doctors follows her—at least five of them—and it's not even the Monday ward round. I tug out my earbuds and lean against the wall.

I hear the door of Room 2 pushed open. I hear shoes arranging themselves inside. Soon, the solid clicking of Dr. Aneta's heels cuts through them.

The last time there were that many doctors in my room

they were celebrating the success of my first treatment with cupcakes and handshakes before ushering me back to the real world. Perhaps Mia's chemo finished early and she won't need the fifth cycle. Perhaps she's luckier than I imagined.

After lashing out at me two days ago, she hasn't bothered to make contact, so neither have I. What's the point?

"How are things, Zac?" I hadn't realized Nina had come in.

"Just stretching my hammies," I say, pushing against the wall.

Beneath my sweatpants, my legs are pale and thin, but they remember what it's like to run.

"Well, I'm in the mood for playing COD." Nina turns on the Xbox.

I make my way to bed. "After weeks of humiliation, you think you can beat me now?"

"It's my last chance."

But I shake my head. "Tomorrow," I say. I want to listen to the speech that will start at any moment. I doubt there'll be cupcakes for Mia. I reckon the whole staff will be glad to see her go.

Nina switches on my TV. "*Happy Feet* is on. I love *Happy Feet*, don't you?"

A penguin dances across the screen, but its tapping isn't quick enough or loud enough to block out what happens next door. It's not a farewell speech. There are no hip-hip-hoorays.

"Mia, listen." Her mother's voice.

"*Listen*, Mia." Dr. Aneta.

"No."

"What's going on?" I ask Nina, who's trying to turn up the volume with my remote.

Nina says, "It's not working," and I don't know if she means the remote or Mia's treatment.

"No," says Mia, again and again. And it breaks my heart. "No."

"We told you this was likely. You *knew* this," Dr. Aneta is saying. "A limb salvage is standard procedure—the *only* procedure now."

"Try more."

"You've had four cycles already. More won't shrink it. Listen, Mia—"

"Mia, listen—"

For a tumor like hers, surgery is a good option: a clean option. When the tumor's removed and a new bone is grafted, her odds skyrocket. But the leg will take ages to heal, longer than the six weeks left till her formal. There'll be months of rehab and a scar.

"Ten or fifteen centimeters," Dr. Aneta says. "Twenty at most."

I wouldn't mind a twenty-centimeter scar up my leg if it meant scooping out all of my cancer. But then, I'm not Mia.

"There'll be no weight-bearing for some time. You'll have a wheelchair—"

"Like a cripple?"

"Like a person who's had surgery."

"I'm not going to my formal in a fucking wheelchair. It can wait till after."

If this was taking place in a children's hospital there would be a team of empathetic staff on standby to say things like *We know the formal is important to you and we don't want you to go in a wheelchair, but in the long run you'll feel so much better. And the scar won't be so bad. We'll get a plastic surgeon. In a year, no one will even notice.*

But we're not in a children's ward and these doctors aren't interested in vanity. That's why Dr. Aneta laughs—not in cruelty, but in disbelief.

"Mia, this isn't a game. If it's left much longer, you'll lose the leg. Worse."

"I don't *care.*"

"Mia, you have to—" says her mum.

But Dr. Aneta cuts her off. "I've booked the surgery for tomorrow morning. The sooner it's done, the more chance there is to save the leg. After that, you'll need more chemo—"

"More?"

"Four more rounds as a safeguard. I can time it so you have leave for the formal, but a wheelchair will be better than crutches. Surgery's at nine, so you have to start fasting now, all right? Will you want sleeping tablets for tonight?"

"I want another *opinion.*"

"I'll leave some here, then, just in case. If you need something stronger, call a nurse."

And with that, the doctors exit the room and file past my door. Music I don't recognize comes belting through the wall, and the song is so loud and hard that it forces Mia's mum from the room as well. A minute later, I watch her dart from the entrance seven stories down, straight-lining for the parking lot.

"I didn't realize how thin these walls were," Nina says,

reluctantly switching off the TV. "You want me to ask her to turn the music down?"

"You feel that brave?"

"Not really."

"It's okay," I say. "Let her be."

10
Zac

The breath is faint on my neck when I register it. A hand is on my shoulder. Too soft to be real.

Am I dreaming? Has a spirit come for me after all?

Behind me, a chest rises and falls. I draw out my own breaths to match. I'm not afraid. If it's a spirit, it's a kind one. A spirit with small hands.

But do spirits wear socks?

Fabric is pressed against my heels. Knees nestle into the backs of mine. I open my eyes in the darkness.

"Mum?" Perhaps my anxious mother's come a day early. But I doubt she'd crawl into bed beside me.

The hand is smaller than my mum's. The breath reminds me of a vanilla milkshake.

I feel a pulse in my foot. Why does the body do that? Why, sometimes, does a body part remind you that blood's beating under the skin in places other than the heart?

Then I realize it's hers. Her pulse beats through the sock and tells me she's alive too.

The blankets cover us both. There are two blankets. How long has she been here?

"Mia?"

But she's sleeping deeply, too distant to reach. I'm aware of all the parts of her that rest against me.

I lengthen my breaths, making them slow and full.

And that's all I know.

• • •

I stretch by the window and check out the cloudless sky that I'll soon be under. I scan the horizon with the knowledge that Mum is on her way and in five hours I'll be heading to that southerly point in the distance, leaving all this brick behind. Soon there'll be no more bed that reclines in three ways, no call button, and no blue blankets.

Blankets. There are two of them. And long hair on my pillow.

A current forks through me.

It *happened*. It was her. With her milky breath and fingers curled around my shoulder. It was real.

I grip my door handle for the first time in forty-nine days and turn it clockwise. I pull it toward me, then poke my head into the corridor. The length of it makes me giddy. I lean further out with a shoulder, then my chest.

Nina spots me. "Zac! Go back in. You need your final obs."

"Oh, come on, I'm going home soon."

"Then you can wait." She's trying to hide the card they've been signing for me.

I send a bare foot onto the linoleum and shift my weight

onto it. The corridor is wider and shinier than I remember. I smell cinnamon toast. There are trolleys along the walls and framed paintings I'd never noticed.

"Zac."

But I'm scampering along the wall, past the curtained windows, to the door with a 2 on it.

Knock.

"Zac!"

"I just want to say goodbye." The door whooshes open when I push it.

Room 2 might be a mirror image of mine, but it's cold and empty. Even the bed's gone. There's nothing but an iPod dock on the bed stand and the word *FASTING* on the whiteboard above.

Nina's voice is behind me. "She's gone, Zac."

"Gone?"

"We wheeled her to Six-A. Now get back to your prison cell for the final countdown." She tries maneuvering me around, but I hold tight to the door frame.

"What's that?" I ask.

Nina's eyes sweep the room before settling on the object. She walks across, picks it up, and turns it over. A plastic ladybug has come free of its hair clip. In Nina's palm it's just a cheap, silly beetle with six indented black spots. I see she's too tired, too kind, too young for this.

"I didn't hear her go," I say.

Nina lets the ladybug drop into the lined bin, then hooks her arm through mine.

"Come on, Zac. Let's get you home."

PART TWO
And

11
Zac

". . . and this year it goes to . . . Zac Meier."

I stop chewing. Was that my name?

"Go on," says Mum. "Shake a leg."

Evan kicks me under the table. "You got an award, dick-head."

Sure enough, two hundred eyeballs are zeroing in on me. From the makeshift stage, Macka's calling me up like I'm a prize puppy.

"That's it, Zac. Come on."

What the hell?

I look to Bec. *An award? For what?* But she, Mum, Dad, and Evan are clapping along with everyone else. I gulp what remains of my bread roll and ketchup.

Players and parents shift their knees as I weave to the front of the hall, scouring my memory for whatever I've done to deserve an end-of-season cricket award. Fielding outer from a camping chair?

I've been out of the hospital for fourteen weeks, and in that time I've only played four matches. Everyone's seen how shit my bowling's been. My fielding wasn't too bad, on the one occasion the ball came within a meter of me. And my batting? I wasn't even allowed. The reality is, I don't deserve a free Coke, let alone the trophy gripped in Macka's hairy hand.

Then it hits me: Best Team Player? Seriously? It's a sympathy vote at the best of times, rewarding good humor and "effort," as opposed to any real skill. Everyone above the age of ten knows it's a consolation prize. For once, I'm glad that my old mates aren't around to witness this.

Macka grabs me as I reach the top step. From here, I see the sweat beads on his forehead and the moist ellipses spreading out from his armpits. It's embarrassing how much he relishes this.

Macka turns me to face the crowd, holding me in case I run. Sympathetic faces shine up at me.

"Many of you wouldn't know it, but Zac was the kind of athlete who could have gone a number of ways: hockey, basketball, soccer, rugby. It didn't matter the shape or size of the ball—Zac knew what to do with it. He always had good hands."

Eyes go searching for my hands, so I push them deep into my jeans pockets.

"Football was a passion, but after he started feeling . . . not so flash . . . last year, I convinced him to spend more time with the 'gentleman's game.' Remember, Zac?"

How can I forget? Football wore me out, so I had to do something else with my afternoons. It was either cricket or swimming. And who'd choose swimming?

"Good hands, good speed, and a heart as big as Phar Lap's. Even when Zac got . . . the bad news . . . he'd still turn up. When he could."

Macka's too clumsy for this. *Get back to the novelty awards,* I want to tell him. *Start on desserts—the mini pavlovas are getting soggy over there.* If he drops the "c" bomb, I'm legging it.

"But he's pulled through—again—and demonstrated real character, on and off the field. He even showed up to training on the day of his eighteenth birthday, cake and all. He's a real team player, our Zac."

I'd love to stuff the trophy into Macka's big mouth, but his next words come out choked up anyway.

"We're all proud of you, Zac. Even when you were in the hospital, you'd be on the Facebook, checking our results and giving *us* encouragement. A real battler. No one deserves this award more than you."

And there it is—the final, backhanded compliment.

I give two sarcastic thumbs-up, snatch the trophy, then jump off the stage. I take the side door and keep on going. I jog across the floodlit field, past the pitch, the semicircular soccer markings and the football posts, aiming for beyond the field where floodlights can't find me. Then I chuck the trophy as far as I can into the unlit national park where by day mountain bikers bump over rocks and grass-tree stumps. Tomorrow, there'll be a new obstacle for them to avoid.

I lean over to catch my breath. Each exhalation is a quick, cold punch in the dark. I'm clear of leukemia, I've got new marrow, so why does this have to follow me? Best Team fucking Player? I don't want charity votes or pity prizes. I don't want a big deal made out of just showing up.

"If that's how you throw, I'm surprised they gave you anything."

Bec. I should've known she'd follow.

"Macka—"

"Macka's a knob. You know that."

"Yeah. But still . . ." I spit and it tastes of ketchup. "He shouldn't have said that. I just want to be . . ."

"Normal?"

"Yeah."

"You are, apart from when you're hurling trophies onto the Bibbulmun Track and muttering to yourself."

"Besides that."

"Want to go back? There's chocolate mousse."

It used to be my favorite, but now it's considered too risky for my immune system, along with a dozen other things. Custard. Soft cheeses. Soft-serve ice cream. Cold meats. Swimming pools. Saunas. Dust spores. Alcohol. I wasn't even allowed one of the barbecued sausages.

"Raw eggs," I remind her. "I can't eat it."

"Neither can I." She rubs her seven-month baby belly.

With her other hand, she rubs my back while I take in sharp jabs of air, glad of the dark.

12
Mia

It's dark. Thank god.

There are no street lights. The moon's behind clouds. Even the car's interior light is broken. I'm glad Rhys has brought us back to King's Park, across from the spot where we first made out. That time, we skipped the movie and drove up here. We admired the twinkling view, but not for long.

Tonight, Rhys parks on the forest side of the road, facing the trees. I'm glad; it's even darker here.

His car smelled of new leather that first night. I got a brain-freeze finishing my Slurpee in a hurry, afraid of spilling it. The radio played, and when that Lady Gaga song came on, Rhys grinned and took off his hat. He checked his hair in the mirror before shifting us both into the back. There was a blanket there, ready. His boot kicked the interior light and it cracked, making him swear, making me laugh. His kiss was rough and cold, Coke and raspberry. His stubble scoured my neck, my breasts, my thighs, leaving a rash that stayed for days.

Tonight, he's tacos and aftershave. I peel off my top and guide his hand to my new bra. I hold his fingers there, wanting him to feel the beaded bow in the middle. I move his other palm to the flat of my stomach, sliding his fingers down to my jeans, then underneath, to the start of the matching undies. I want him to remember the feel of me. "God you're hot," he used to moan.

"Wait." He stops. "I don't think . . ."

Rhys isn't supposed to think. He's supposed to sigh, his back a slick of sweat, grabbing and grunting on the tidy leather seats. "Christened it," he said after that first time. "The car," he clarified, grinning and pulling his hat back on.

But now he puts his hands back on the steering wheel. He concentrates on the forest as if he's a fucking botanist all of a sudden.

"What?"

"We broke up," he says.

"'We'?" He was the one who let my calls go to voice mail. He was the one who stopped answering texts. No, *we* didn't break up. *He* backed out.

"I can't—"

"What? Fuck me?"

"No. Yes."

I hadn't intended to go all the way, just far enough to get him interested. "You don't think I'm . . ." What's the word I need? *Pretty? Fuckable?* "Anymore?"

"Don't do this to me."

I grab his hand again and push it down my jeans. I want him to want me. My other hand unzips his fly. Even when he nudges me away, I touch him the way he likes. I want him to grow hard and hot in my hand as proof that I'm still sexy, that I can still make him moan.

But he doesn't. He grips my wrist and stops me, all the while staring into bushland.

"There's no point."

I laugh. He never did get irony.

"You're an asshole." I grab my backpack from the floor and grope the back seat for my T-shirt and crutches. I pull the shirt on. "And a coward." I throw open the car door and swivel into the cool night air. When I stand, my crutches crunch into gravel.

"Don't be stupid. Mia. I'll drive you home."

"Home?"

"Well, where? Erin's?"

"No." I'm not going back there. Her mum corners me with questions, thinking she already knows the answers.

"Or your other friend," he suggests. "That skinny one."

He doesn't offer his flat, at the back of his parents' house, even though he used to smuggle me in there before. Before.

"Screw you," I say, pivoting and slamming the door of his precious car. "I'm too good for you anyway." I punch at the door with the solid end of a crutch. A panel gives way, so I do it again. "Too hot for *you*, Rhys. Everyone says that."

My brain corrects me. *Said*, not *says*. Everyone *said* that.

"I'm still hot, Rhys. I'm still fucking hot."

He reverses, and I hit the car again. I want to smash his windows, smash him, too.

Dirt and gravel detonate as he spins and speeds away, leaving me with two crutches and a backpack in a dark, dark forest.

I'm glad it's dark. It's so dark, I can't even see myself.

13
Zac

No one mentions my award on the drive home, and by the time we're in front of the TV, ice cream bowls in our laps, it's ancient history. During *Better Homes and Gardens*, Mum, Dad, and Evan talk about olives. I'm grateful for the way they act like tonight never happened, like everything is normal.

On cue, Bec calls my name through the door. It's Friday night and the shit needs clearing, after all. She has a driver hooked over her left shoulder and a three-iron over her right. I pull on my boots and grab flashlights; then we follow the beams past the houses, the store, and up along the paved path to the pens, where sheep and goats form woolly clumps, settling into sleep. Bec shines her light over the ewes, checking if any are close to birthing.

She swings her light to the alpaca pen too, where five are sleeping, their front feet folded beneath them. The other three sneer and move away. Even the original alpaca, Daisy, scowls.

We hook the flashlights to fence posts to light up the path.

Then Bec lines her club against some pellets and shuffles into position.

Roo poos are perfect missiles, dry and compact enough to get good air, even when fresh. Sheep and goats, on the other hand, leave stodgy, moist mounds that explode on impact. Sheep shit golf never ends well, so we leave them in the pens along with their owners.

It's the wild roo shit that annoys Mum because it gets everywhere—in the pens, the shop's entrance, the customer restrooms, the new pavers, under the seats and along the main walkway, from one end of the petting farm to the other. Roos can jump any fence to help themselves to feed, leaving enough ammunition to keep us busy each Friday, clearing the way for weekend visitors.

Pregnancy may have altered Bec's stance, but her swing remains smooth and fast, sending each pellet over pens and most of the olive trees below. I reckon she harbors dreams of becoming a pro golfer. The media would love her, asking for recounts of her training regime: a thousand pellets every week.

"Evan's going to get his heart broken," she says.

"Again? Where's this one from?"

"France. Have you seen her? Twenty-one and supercute."

"So Dad's hiring French girls to pick instead of me? You know what that does for my ego?"

"There are six backpackers, Zac. She's not just for you."

"Shit, it's not like I'll chop off a limb."

"Doctor's orders."

The comprehensive "So You've Had a Bone Marrow Transplant: What Now?" booklet has been memorized by everyone in my family, including Evan, whose reading is usually limited to *Zoo Weekly*. Thanks to this booklet I'm banned from contact sports, running, dirt biking, physical labor, and operating mechanical equipment for twelve months. Homework, unfortunately, is deemed safe.

"It's picking olives, Bec, not motocross."

"Anyway, I'll need your help with feeds. Dad'll be busy with pickers, and there's a busload of tourists coming. First day of school vacation . . ." she adds, as if it's slipped my mind. As if.

"How am I supposed to meet a hot backpacker if I'm up here with toddlers?"

"I'll send out spies," she says. "Actually, there *is* a German picker . . ."

"Nuh. Given my marrow, that'd feel . . . incestuous."

"There might be an Italian. Or a cute Kiwi. I'll investigate." Across the flashlight beam, my sister's scheming. "You could do with a fling."

Bec's got no idea of the surplus of girls in my life already. At school I'm a novelty—an older guy come back to repeat a year. In study periods, they beckon me over to their desks, asking for help with topics I should already know. But there's more to it than study: girls can sniff out vulnerability. I see the way they look at my scars. They're careful with me, as if I'm covered in warning labels. ACHTUNG. FRAGILE.

But it's not gentleness I'm after. Or sympathy.

I mis-swing and a pellet shoots off at an angle, rattling the roof of the coop and setting chickens into a flap.

"Just a fling," Bec says, trying to read my thoughts. "It's not on your banned list . . ."

"A setup from my sister? Awesome."

"You'd want to work on your personality, though, considering your sporting ability's gone to pot."

I smack a crap so hard, it whistles into the dark like an unexploded firework. It feels amazing.

"Lucky," Bec says.

Then she leans on a gate and lets me whack the rest of them, every satisfying one.

• • •

Hey Zac

How's it going, champ? Happy belated 18th. Life back to normal yet?

Listen, you gotta become an electrician. Working three days a week is the duck's nuts. Heading to Wedge Island this weekend for annual Bombing Range trip. Classic.

My 9-foot longboard's waiting. Next time you're in Perth, you gotta try. Birthday treat. Catch ya then,

Cam

I tap my pen at one of the new postcards advertising The Good Olive! Olive Oil and Petting Farm. I wish I could tell Cam that life's brilliant, but I can't.

"This could change things," Patrick had said on my last day in the hospital. "You've been stuck in a room for forty-nine days—"

"Thirty-three with my *mum*."

"Yes. What was I saying?"

"Change."

"Yes. You might."

"Look at this . . . Do you think my hair's growing back orange?"

"Emotional changes," Patrick said. "Not just physical, Zac."

"I *am* emotional about it." I'd laughed, skimming a hand across my head. "Leukemia twice, German marrow, and now a born-again redhead. That's bloody unfair."

Then Mum arrived and I grabbed my bag and bolted. The elevator dropped us to the ground floor, where we followed the green arrows to the exit. Outside, the width of the world dizzied me. No walls! Instead there was freedom. Cars. Ticket machines. Traffic lights. Traffic. The blue of the ocean. Eighty kilometers an hour. Mum and I kept the windows down all the way home and I couldn't suck in enough air.

And when the car finally pulled in to home, with its new and improved THE GOOD OLIVE! OLIVE OIL AND PETTING FARM sign, I could smell chicken shit from fifty meters and it was sweeter than anything. I knew better than to admit this, of course — my sanity was under scrutiny as it was. Then my Jack Russell barked and tried to slobber me, but Evan held him back while the others hugged me in turn, and I felt like the luckiest German beer wench to have ever lived. To ever be allowed to live again.

I went back to school, though I'd sleep through periods five and six. I was even grateful for homework because drawing demographic data and analyzing economic plans meant I was normal, like every other year-twelve student with deadlines and exams, with my life moving forward in a solid black line from A to B to C.

Which is why I don't want this April vacation to happen. Without the structure of school, time doesn't function like a solid black line at all. Time plays tricks. It can mess with you. When you least expect it, time can loop back on itself, like a giant rubber band. Time can tap you on the shoulder. If it wants to, it can pick you right up and fling you back into Room 1, with its needles and bleach and nausea and Mia. Mia. Shit. Where is she? Is she okay?

That tap on the wall. Her angry, desperate tap and uncensored questions.

Has her hair grown back? Did she go to her formal in a wheelchair? Has she moved on, the way she's supposed to, laughing and flirting in the mall on weekends? Is she showing off her scar with pride yet? Has she forgotten about me, the way she's meant to? The way I was supposed to forget about her?

But I don't know because she's not on Facebook. By the time I'd arrived home and had the "Welcome Back, Zac" dinner, then found a quiet hour to log on—Was I dreaming or did you join me in the night? Are you a sleepwalker, or did you mean to? How did it go today?—her Facebook profile had been pulled. At first I thought she'd unfriended me, but when I searched her name, I realized she wasn't anywhere. She'd erased herself.

How can you share someone's secrets, sent back and forth in the quiet of early mornings, but not know basic stuff like the suburb they live in or their phone number? How can someone vanish from your life so easily?

I turn the blank postcard over in my hands. What would I write, if I knew her address? Would it sound casual, like Cam's? *Thought I'd drop you a line . . .* Or would I tell her more? That normal isn't normal anymore, and that I don't know if it ever will be. That I'm still in semi-quarantine. That I'm afraid of school vacations, and spending two whole weeks on my own.

Mum opens my door. Since the hospital, she no longer bothers to knock. "Do you want to have a party?"

"Now?"

"Next week. Get the relatives over, and your friends." She stirs the contents of her bowl in slow motion, already planning it. "Matthew and Alex would come. And Rick . . ."

"They're away," I remind her, taken off to Perth or beyond, for work or study. "Didn't you have ice cream already?"

"Your new friends at school. They'll come, won't they?"

"Depends on the booze."

Mum points her spoon at the "Bone Marrow Transplant" booklet pinned to the corkboard above my desk. Alcohol: banned substance number two.

"For them," I say.

"Maybe just the family, then. A barbecue. It'd be nice to celebrate your hundred-day benchmark, don't you think?"

A party is the last thing I want. If one hundred days of "normal" is to be celebrated, isn't that kind of missing the point?

I say yes, mostly for Mum's sake, but partly for my own. A party might give me something else to think about.

Something other than her.

14
Mia

The cabbie gives me a discount but it's not the "You're a cute chick I want to impress" discount. It's a "You're on crutches" discount. "Mascara's down your face" discount. Sympathy. Shit, I'll take it if it means seven extra bucks in my pocket. I need it more than him.

I press the doorbell three times and rub my cheeks with the sleeve of my sweater. It's Shay's dad who opens the door. He puts on frameless glasses, checks the clock on the wall, then inspects my face under the sensor light.

"Sorry, Mr. W.—is Shay here?"

"Maya?"

"Mia."

He nods, remembering. It's been a while.

"You're blond."

"Yeah. You like?"

"Very nice. What have you done to yourself?" He's looking at the crutches.

"Volleyball injury. Stupid, huh? Shay said I could crash here. If I needed to."

"Tonight?"

"Yeah." I hold up my backpack. "I know it's late. Sorry."

He checks the clock again, scratching his chest. "They're inside."

"'They'?"

He shrugs. "End of term."

Shit. Shay I could handle. A group's something else.

"I thought you quit school."

"I went part-time, for the diploma. I'll be catching up next year . . ." I have answers for everything.

"You're okay, then? You're not in any . . . trouble?"

I snort as if it's a joke. "Me?"

Shit, if I started thinking about the trouble I'm in, I'd choke. Maybe I should just turn and leave. Catch a ride with another sympathetic cabbie. But where?

"Well, come in," he says. "It's late."

In the living room, furniture is draped with clothes, blankets, and girls I know well. Chloe is on the couch and Erin and Fee are lying on mattresses. Shay stands by the television with DVDs in hand. They pause for too long when I enter, checking each other for approval. What unsaid things are passing between them? How much do they know?

I wish I were a ghost. I would just float out of here. I wouldn't want to haunt them.

Shay drops the DVDs and steps over the mattresses to hug me. I hold on to my crutches, unable to hug back.

"Mia! You remembered."

. . .

The end-of-term movie marathon was the brainchild of Shay and me in year eight. It was just the two of us then, scoffing Pods and Twisties and hot chocolates, allowing other girls to join us if they met our criteria. Over the years, Tim Tams replaced Pods. Baileys was added to milk. These nights became stuff of legend, inspiring guys to drive laps of the street and shout out things to embarrass us. They were the reward for ten boring weeks of classes with teachers who kept us separated.

In the bathroom, Shay hands me a cleansing wipe. My reflection shocks me; I keep forgetting I'm someone else. Mascara smudges onto the wipe.

"I would have invited you," she says, inspecting her eyebrows in the mirror, "but I thought you'd gone. You didn't reply to my texts."

"I've been with Rhys. You know what he's like."

"You still going to Sydney?"

"Tomorrow," I say. "My aunt's expecting me. I'm catching a bus."

"You realize you could fly."

I smile at her. "Where's the adventure in that?" Besides, flying would mean showing my ID.

Shay's watching my reflection now. "It's not the same without you. Are you coming back?"

I shrug.

"Mr. Perlman says if you've quit school, your mum needs to come in and sign something."

"She did already. Relax."

My face clear, I turn toward the room, where the others have rearranged the mattresses and sleeping bags. They're in sweatpants and T-shirts, but Chloe wears a cami and Peter Alexander boxer shorts. Her legs are tanned and toned and freakishly long. She bends to pluck a Tim Tam from a packet, then puts it between her teeth and gives me a chocolaty smile. She used to envy me, once.

"Mia, you can have this one," Fee says, pointing her glossy red toenails at the mattress closest to the bathroom. Since when did Fee get invited to movie marathons? "In case you need to get up in the night."

She's trying to be tactful. The last time someone asked about my ankle I told her to fuck off. Then I took off.

Chloe slides onto a mattress with Erin and the two of them decide on the order of viewing. Comedy, horror, comedy, romance, horror. I'm alert to every word, not wanting to miss a whisper.

"Fuck." Shay is still in the bathroom, pinching the skin on her cheek. "Pimple. See?"

"No," I say, swinging closer. There's nothing there.

"Brandon's party is tomorrow. Erin!" she yells. "You got that tea tree stuff?"

I laugh. It's funny. "Shay, there's nothing there."

"I'm not turning up to Brandon's with a zit on me."

She squeezes her cheek and I realize she's serious. Erin runs in with the tea tree gel, applying and fussing as if this emergency is real. As if it matters.

I feel I'm watching through a glass bowl. Is this how life is for them? Is this how it was for me?

Am I the fish, or are they?

Through the night, the four girls switch positions on mattresses and pass around food. I only eat the salted popcorn: gummy bears give me stomach cramps and chocolate still reminds me of wax.

Chloe notices. "Are you on a diet, Mia?"

A diet? I'd forgotten the word.

"You shouldn't be. You're skinny." Shay says this like it's a compliment.

I eat a waxy Tim Tam for the sake of it, then take another. I'd eat anything to keep their attention off me. I'm hoping they'll just shut up and focus on the movies, but their conversation drags on and on: *Mr. Perlman sucks; I'm going to get implants; I hate my split ends; Joel's too good for Beth; I want a tattoo here, but I don't know what; does Chloe's brother like me?; my nails keep chipping; can you see my cellulite?; I've got to lose five pounds before Brandon's formal.*

Their dialogue is broken with laughs and farts and snorts. I feel like I've lived this night before. Even the horror film, when finally played, is predictable. Horror? Not even close.

They are the fish, I realize. I see them in their spotless bowl, swimming around in shallow circles. I used to cherish our group above all else, protecting our precious in-jokes from others who looked on in envy. These girls — and the other half-dozen guys and girls who ruled the bench outside D Block — were my world. We were real and loud and fearless. Our histories are etched into the wooden slats of that bench.

But now it's me who's looking in, though not with envy. How to lose ten pounds in a week? I could tell them how to lose five pounds in a day. Split ends—are they kidding? And who the fuck cares about pimples? When your scalp itches like mine, your leg throbs like hell, and food still makes you want to spew, you stop looking for pimples that aren't there. You stop laughing at jokes that aren't funny. You stop thinking of "skinny" as praise.

When I pretend to sleep, I hear the whispers not meant for me: *Did you invite her? Why has she been such a bitch? You were just trying to help. Rhys deserves better. Like Brooke.*

After the last movie ends and whispers turn to breaths, I check my phone. There's a new text from Mum.

> I know uve been here. $130 missing from jar. Come sort it
> out or leave for good. No more sneaking. Grow up!

I delete it and put the phone down. The time pulses: 2:59 a.m. Three a.m. It makes me wonder if he's awake too. Zac. It's been more than three months. Long enough for him to forget me.

I hope he's sleeping. I hope he's not lying awake like me, too pathetic for tears. I hope he's sleeping so deep that not even dreams can find him.

Fuck, I need to *think.* Plan A relied on my mum being a normal person. Plan B expected my boyfriend to be a man. Plan C was Shay and other girlfriends who always promised to do anything for me.

What I need now is a Plan D. *D* for *desperate. D* for *do or die.*

• • •

Before dawn I pick my way through them. The ends of my crutches find spaces between smooth limbs and curled palms. I step over long hair splashed across plump pillows. They sleep like babies. I'm not mad at them. It's not their fault they don't know better.

I swing above them and into the kitchen. Near the microwave is a handbag and, in it, a red wallet. There's a cropped photo of a happy young Shay, and two hundred bucks.

"Sorry," I whisper. Another quick escape. Another mark against my name. This time, I'll have to go further. I'll go to Sydney, for real. As Mum said, *Sort it out or leave for good.*

I catch a bus to Central Station, then buy a ticket for as far as I can afford. It'll have to do, for now.

A woman vacates the front seat for me. RESERVED FOR DISABLED PASSENGERS, the sign says. I take it.

I hold tight to my backpack. Inside is my cell and charger, iPod and headphones, lip-gloss, mascara, foundation, two T-shirts, sweatpants, five pairs of undies, deodorant, driver's license, $416.80, a tube of hand sanitizer, a tub of Vitamin E moisturizer, and half a pack of OxyContin.

The bus shakes as it warms itself up and lurches us into the cold blue city. In every street, I see the ghost of myself staring back.

I wish I'd packed a pillow to lean against the window. I wish I had more painkillers. I wish I had more money.

More than anything, I wish I had a better fucking plan.

15
Zac

"Morning, sunshine."

Bec hands me a bucket and a long pair of gloves. I know I'm supposed to wear them while working with animals, but do they have to be pink?

She notices my reaction. "Would you prefer Dad's blue ones?"

"God, no." We both know where those have been—Dad's approach to animal husbandry is disturbingly hands-on. I snatch the pink gloves, pull wellies over my sweatpants, and follow her.

Our buckets chink with bottles of warm milk as we make our way up past the pens of goats and sheep. Most are awake, munching placidly on grass.

We get a noisier reception in the hayshed. In one cage, week-old lambs bleat and push at each other, greedy and desperate. In another, three-day-old kids jig on back legs. They're stupidly cute, with gummy eyes and snotty nostrils. Their entire bodies shake in anticipation of a feed, making me laugh. It's almost worth getting out of bed for.

Bec offers bottles to the lambs so I take the others for the kids, who pull so hard at the teats I have to hold my ground. For a few minutes there's nothing but a choir of wet sucking. Yeah, this is worth getting out of bed for. But as soon as the bottles run dry, there's total baa-ing, bleating madness.

The birds are even louder. I unlatch the doors and roosters hustle past, crowing insults at the world. *Short-man syndrome*, Bec calls it as they strut by. In the coop, chickens flap and squawk, as if this is a rude shock rather than the usual morning ritual. They flee the cage and scatter themselves across the hay-shed and out to the grass, where they peck at leftover grains, and shit like they own the place.

I move from cage to cage, refilling containers with fresh water and scattering handfuls of hay.

There have been births in the night—I find two tiny guinea pigs and four fluffy chicks. There's been a death, too—the week-old rabbit that lasted longer than anyone expected. I lift out the runt and its siblings fill the gap.

The sound of an engine cuts through the commotion. It's Dad who's driving the pickup, towing a trailer loaded with rakes, tubs, ladders, and ground sheets. On an ATV, Evan rumbles close to the hayshed, sending up a cloud of dust, crap, and disgruntled poultry.

"Nice gloves," he shouts, before doing a doughnut and scooting down toward the olive orchard. I give him a pink finger, but I reckon the intended impact is lost. What an ass.

"Ignore him," says Bec.

"He doesn't have to rub it in." Of all the jobs on the farm, picking is the best. Picking means long days of mucking around with Dad and backpackers with nicknames like Beaker, Suni, Giraffe, and Wookie. Picking means setting nets under trees and raking at branches until the nets turn black with olives. Evan will inevitably show off with the pneumatic rake, shooting olives like bullets into unsuspecting faces. Then, on hands and knees, they'll all pull out twigs, leaves, and rotten olives, and share stories from around the world. I'd give anything to be down there, hearing the first squeal of whichever girl mistakes a roo pellet for an olive, and the first yelp of whichever guy gets spooked by a frill-neck lizard. I want to see the tray overflowing again and again, to look back on an empty row and see what we've achieved, then end the day with aching muscles and new friends made and the sound of the Oliomio processor that goes into the night, Mum and Dad at the controls, sharing a bottle of wine to celebrate the first crush of the season.

But I'm stuck up here with fluffy animals and pink rubber gloves. I scan the sheep cages for babies or dead bodies, but see neither. Either way, they'd have to be removed: newborns need to be taken away from opportunistic foxes; corpses have to be hidden from the sight of tourists. There were complaints last year when half a lamb was discovered by hysterical children. Visitors prefer their lambs to bleat, not decompose, apparently.

A car arrives early. Doors slam and kids squeal.

"Good luck." I hand Bec the wheelbarrow. School vacations are tough on everyone, especially the animals, who get squeezed like toys.

I go in the other direction, swinging the dead rabbit up to

the northern end of the farm. NO ENTRY, the gate warns, separating the farm from the bushland next door. The Sydney-based owners have left the property the way they bought it twenty years ago: a thick mess of bottle brushes, she-oaks, marris, and grass trees.

I figure if I bring dead bodies to the vixen, she won't be so tempted by the living. I know she'll be watching me. She would have smelled the warm runt hanging from my glove. She'll be keen — she's got babies of her own to feed.

I wonder if she can smell me too, the way the girls at school can: not death, but weakness. Vulnerability. I wonder if she senses I'm not as strong as I should be, caught in limbo between sickness and health. ACHTUNG. FRAGILE.

When the fox comes, she's low and smooth. She watches me carefully, even though she knows I won't hurt her. She recognizes me from before, then pads farther out, dissecting me with her eyes. She knows all about me, it seems.

I lob the runt and it hits the ground between us.

"Go on, have it. But stay away from the pens."

She snatches the rabbit and scampers back through the bush. It's a simple transaction, without sadness or guilt. It's just the food chain made real.

I've been told not to think about death, but it's not easy. The booklet advises me, *Recite positive affirmations. Stay in the present. Make plans for the future. Keep yourself busy.* I shake the fence just to hear it rattle.

I'm well, I tell myself. *I'm fine. And so is she.*

• • •

"And that one over there is a baby." It's Bec's voice that eventually finds me. "You wouldn't know it to look at him, but he's a friendly beast with a gentle nature. He'll eat a pie right out of your hand."

In a huddle, tourists snicker. Children giggle, enjoying the joke.

Bec smiles smugly. "Though I'd recommend keeping your distance. His breath can be bad in the mornings."

I scratch my bum theatrically and jump off the gate. I walk past them, letting myself into the emu pen to collect the three green eggs that have rolled to the fence. I hand them to Bec, then leave her to supervise the feeding of the emus.

"Keep your palm flat!" I hear from the hayshed. I snap off the pink gloves, drop them in a bin, and head for home, passing the shop and alpaca pen. Mum's walking toward me with a tray of hot scones.

"Feel like making twenty cups of tea?"

"So tempting," I say, "but *Pride and Prejudice* is waiting." English homework has got to be useful for something.

"Still?"

"I can't rush it. It's not like your *Fifty Shades of Grey*." But Mum's already out of earshot, the scones steaming behind her.

Sometimes that's all it takes—a smell—to lasso me back to Room 1. A hand curling over my shoulder and Mia curving into the back of me. Her vanilla breath in the night.

It stops me in my tracks. *Breathe*, I remind myself. *Stay in the present.*

A joey sidles up to me and sniffs at my fingers. I show her an empty palm and give her a scratch behind the ears, even though I'm not supposed to. When she's bored with me, she jumps toward the old shed and sniffs inside.

Crammed with fifteen years of useless junk, the shed is a danger zone of outdated farm equipment and crap left over from the last owner. There'd be rats and rusty nails and other hazards best avoided by a person with a compromised immune system.

So I go in and let my eyes adjust. A small stepladder sways when I climb it. From here, I see stacks of timber, reminding me of year-ten Woodworking. I used planks like these to build a coffee table for Mum. It took me a term and a half to finish it, and then I built another one for Bec for Christmas. There's good timber going to waste here, but how many coffee tables do people need?

The idea takes shape before my eyes: a baby's crib. Bec hasn't bought one yet, and I know she'd prefer something handmade. Best of all, a baby's crib would be ambitious and time-consuming—exactly the kind of project I need to keep myself in the present.

To keep my mind off her.

16
Mia

I haven't come here for scones.

The animals are cute, granted, but I haven't come here for them either. I'm not a child.

Inside the store, tourists dip cubes of bread into shallow bowls while a woman describes five flavors of oils. It looks like her, a bit slimmer maybe, with dyed hair. She seems nicer than in the hospital, but then, you'd expect her to be nice to customers. She nods at tourists. Makes encouraging comments about the lightness and depth of olive oil. Shit, I haven't come here for any of this.

Yeah, I think it's the mum. But Zac? I'm not sure. He walked right past me before, beside the emus. I didn't care much for them either, with their beady eyes and strong beaks. He wasn't scared, though: he went in with them and came out holding three eggs in his pink gloves.

There's a paved path leading down to a gate with a hand-painted sign, which reads NO ENTRY — RESIDENCE. Just past that, the guy is standing near a shed. A small kangaroo is beside him. Is it Zac? The hair's short and dark. I hadn't expected that. He's better-looking than I'd thought.

I need to get closer, but NO ENTRY, reminds the sign.

I could call out his name, couldn't I? But what if it's not him? I'd look like a dumbass. And what if it is?

He seems too tall. Then again, I never saw him standing.

If I call his name and he turns, what would I shout? *Remember me? The one you lied to?* I wouldn't care who heard me, either. He promised I'd be fine and he was wrong.

But he steps into the shed and out of sight.

Behind me, the driver herds the tour group from the shop and I go too. When he attempts to help me onto the bus, I shrug him off. My crutches drive mud into each carpeted step. He waits until I'm safe in the front seat, then pulls out of the parking lot.

It doesn't matter if it was or wasn't Zac. He wasn't a part of Plan D anyway. He was just a side trip to break up a long day.

• • •

"You can't use that," says the coach driver in town.

I thrust the ticket back at him. "But I bought it this morning."

"It's for a different route," he says, blowing smoke away from me. Why is he smoking so close to a bus, anyway? "Direct. It's not a hop-on, hop-off service."

I laugh at the irony. All I can do these days is hop.

"You should have got the hop-on, hop-off ticket if you wanted to go sightseeing."

"I don't," I say. "I didn't. Look, I'm going to Adelaide, it says, via Albany. Today."

He drops the butt and scuffs it into the cement. I hate it when people do that. Where do they think it's going to go? It pisses me off big-time.

"You can get on board if you're that keen, but I'm heading to Pemberton. That way." He points. "The next coach to Albany doesn't come through till tomorrow—"

"Tomorrow?"

"You should be able to reuse the ticket, but you'd want to ring ahead to see if there's a seat. School vacations and all." He shrugs. "Unlucky."

Fucker. At least he's got something right.

• • •

"You are lucky," the young guy at the hostel tells me.

He's got to be kidding.

"You are lucky there is a bed." His clipped accent is hard to understand. "This time of season there is many fruit pickers." He notices my crutches, then checks my face. I should have put on makeup. "You are picking?"

I hold out twenty-five bucks and tell him I'll return later. I'm not in the mood to spend the afternoon in a communal lounge.

Instead, I go to the main street, where I buy a sandwich and an iced coffee and sit on a bench near a butcher shop. Women spend ages in there. When they come out they stand on the sidewalk and gossip, their chops and sausages sweating through plastic. Stupid fucking people in a stupid fucking town.

Across the road is a police station, its window plastered with photos of missing people. I go and look them over—all these men and women who are dead or pretending to be. Some were last seen before I was born.

My face isn't there. I wonder if Mum's told the cops, the way she'd threatened to. I wonder if they'd bother with a poster for me. If so, what would it say?

Missing: Mia Phillips. Seventeen-year-old female, currently with blond bob. 164 centimeters. Crutches. Needs two more rounds of chemo and immediate medical attention. Suspected of theft and deception. Potentially dangerous.

If a poster ever finds its way down here, I'll be long gone. I've learned a lesson today—no more unplanned detours. Life doesn't favor the curious. No more hopping on or off. No more trying my luck with bus drivers or girlfriends or ex-boyfriends or mothers or doctors or random strangers who once stayed in adjoining hospital rooms and fed me bullshit lies.

Everyone lies. So just take your backpack and go, Mia. Go direct.

Fuck 'em all.

17
Zac

The Oliomio processor clunks to a stop and the night inflates with quiet. I hear my parents creep their way alongside the house. *Shhh,* whispers Dad in the dark. I hear Mum giggle. Glasses clink. They close the front door behind them.

In the processing shed, 6,000 liters of cold-pressed oil will be freshly bottled. It was a decent harvest today, so Evan boasted, with another twelve rows to be picked and crushed tomorrow. It'll happen again in a month with the manzanillos. I'm hoping I can talk my way into it by then.

I sleep with my head beneath the window, the curtain wide open. Even after fourteen weeks out of the hospital, this feels important.

It baffles me how the mess of the universe knows exactly what it's doing, like it was all agreed on thirteen billion years ago and the galaxies have been following the rules ever since. They're all up there, keeping in tempo and making perfect sense, whereas we humans screw up everything in the short time we've got.

I hear footsteps on the grass that shouldn't be there — Mum and Dad are inside and the alpacas should be sleeping by now. Perhaps one's restless from the noisy night. Or it could be Sheba, who's due to give birth soon.

I listen. There are more footsteps, farther away, then a soft grunt and a spit.

I get up and lean my head and chest out of the window, my arms aching from the effort of heaving things around in the shed.

It's Daisy, the old alpaca. "Go to sleep, you tool."

But what I hear next is more human than animal. There's a dull clunk in the darkness, then a flash of light. I see it up by the hayshed. Blue. Twice.

I wrap my quilt around me and hoist myself through the window. My Jack Russell, J.R., is already at my shin, whacking me with his tail. He trails me as I walk barefoot up the path, opening and then closing the gate, but stays behind when I go to the hayshed. The chicken.

Under the orange glow of small heat lamps, babies sleep peacefully in their cages, safe from foxes. They snuffle and dream.

I sneak past them to find the source of the blue flash. On top of a pile of hay, the disc looks like a small UFO, sending beams in each direction. *Blink, flicker, blink.* I'd forgotten about this device, which Dad drags out each cubbing season. It's supposed to scare off vixens, tricking them into believing humans are about.

It worked on me, at least. I gather the quilt tighter, trying to hold it above the dirt as I retrace my steps between pens, through the gate, and back down to the house. Sharp stars mock me. My bare feet are freezing.

I crawl back through my window. Outside, Daisy grunts again.

What an idiot: scared of a blue light. I pull down the window to keep out her whines.

But Daisy's not the only one who's restless. As I stand in my room, the walls suddenly feel too close, the air too quiet. I keep the quilt around me, my ears ringing in the vacuum. There's not a single whir or buzz or hum. Not even a breath.

But then there's a *tap*.

And a face at the window.

I see it and fall, staggering backwards as the past pitches madly, impossibly toward me.

• • •

The girl forces up the window and thrusts out an arm. *Shhh!* her flexed hand warns. *Be still.*

I still myself, my knees and elbows tangled in quilt. I find a breath, then another, while the girl hovers there, silhouetted by stars. Is she human?

The hair is thick and short. Her eyes are large. "Mia?"

She brings a finger to her lips. Her eyes inspect my darkened room, and then her hand swivels and, palm upward, beckons me.

Her skin is cold. I take her forearm to help her through the window but she lands badly and both of us twist and crumple in quilt.

Above me, she's vanilla and ice and fear.

"Mia?" I ask again, though I don't need to.

I crawl free and she draws my blankets around her. Then, without explanation or apology, she rolls to her side, facing my bedroom wall.

I prop myself against the bed frame, wide awake and stunned with wonder.

• • •

I've helped rescue all kinds of animals. For as long as I can remember, Bec and I would pull on boots and jackets and follow Dad to the pickup. How many goats have we pulled free from fences? How many parrots have we wrapped in old towels? Countless cardboard boxes watched over on the rattling drive home.

I've helped rescue plenty, but that's where it ends. It was always Dad who fixed them.

Mum would toss up her arms in despair as another lamb was placed in the oven on low heat, the door left open. Other times, Dad would put on his Speedo and sit in a warm bath, dripping water over a baby alpaca given up for dead by its mother. Its head would loll and loll until eventually it snorted air. Dad believed heat could bring back the dead.

I wonder what he'd say about this: a girl in my room, sleeping as if on an edge.

She seems warmer, at least, but it might only be on the surface. What would Dad do now?

Daylight creeps across her. I watch her slow breaths, aware of my own. Mia—it has to be. Even though her hair's now blond, with too-straight bangs.

Each noise freaks me out. The creak of floorboards in the laundry. Mum? Dad and Evan driving down to the olives. Outside, the crazy clucking of chickens. Bec will be feeding the newborns and she'll be wondering where I am.

I tiptoe to the window and peer through the curtain. I see roosters and chickens pecking by the hayshed. Bec's out of sight.

I let the curtain drop, and when I turn, the girl has one eye watching. Hair veils the rest of her face but she doesn't brush it away.

"Hey."

She says nothing. Just keeps her one eye on me.

I can't match her stare, so I look down at my hands. I don't know what to do with them. What happens now?

"How did—" I begin, then stop. *How* can wait. "Mia?" I ask, needing confirmation. "Are you lost?"

It's stupid. Of course she's not lost. A Perth girl doesn't leave her house, take a wrong turn, and end up on the southern coast of Western Australia.

Quick footsteps come at us and Mia's eyes widen. She sits up. My doorknob rattles.

"Zac, you in there?"

"Yeah," I croak.

"Why is the door locked? You getting up? I'm doing sheets."

But my sheets are wrapped tight around the girl who's eyeing the window as an escape route.

"Can't a guy sleep in?" I call out. "Even God rested on a Sunday."

"*God?* Are you all right, Zac?"

"I'm trying to speed-read chapter seven of *Pride and Prejudice.*"

"Sheets?"

"Nah, thanks. I haven't shat myself in months."

"Male," Mum mutters. "Don't stay in all day—Bec's got her hands full."

We wait for her footsteps to peter out. Mia's back is pressed against the wall.

"Sorry," I say, though I'm not sure why.

Short hair falls on either side of her face and I see it's not the same face that looked through my hospital window. She's not the same girl anymore, and it isn't just the hair.

Her gaze slides across my skin. Without a shirt on, I feel suddenly vulnerable. She's checking me over, her eyes snagging on the scars: the one at my right pec, the old one at my neck, the dots on my inner arms. She knows where to find them. The proof seems to relax her a little.

"It *is* you," she murmurs. "Helga, you look different."

"It's Zac," I say. "Yeah. So do you."

"Your eyes are gray."

"They're more like blue."

"They look gray."

She brushes away her bangs and I run my hands through my own hair, leaving my fingers linked behind my head, the way Dad does when assessing a situation.

Where do I start? This girl's materialized from a white-walled room fourteen weeks in the past, five hundred kilometers away.

"What are you doing here?"

She blinks, looks down at the floorboards.

"Are you okay?"

She starts to speak but her words catch in her throat, as if they've got barbs.

"What's wrong?" I ask, even though I shouldn't.

On my last day in the hospital, when I went to thank Nina one last time, I saw the way she'd pivoted down the corridor and walked in another direction. I suspected then that Mia's surgery hadn't gone well, but what could I do? Mum talked too much on the drive home, as if she'd known, somehow, then pulled into a McDonald's drive-through without prompting, even though my craving for a burger had gone. Later in the day, Mia would be waking, heavy with anesthetic and painkillers and whatever sedatives they could justify. But what would she be waking to? How bad was the scar? I didn't know for sure. And I couldn't ask.

"Sorry," I say.

Her face tightens.

A screen door bangs and Mum calls the chickens to scraps. Soon she'll be getting the till ready in the store. Bec will be checking for newborns and corpses, and I should be helping.

Outside is noisy, but in here, I can't think of what to say. Mia drags my quilt over her head, shrouding herself.

"What do you want? Mia?"

She stays quiet, hidden.

What would Dad do? Walk away? Scoop her up in his arms? She's too big for the oven.

I pull on a T-shirt and walk out of the room. In the kitchen, I make a grilled cheese and tomato with ketchup. While it cools down, I microwave some hot chocolate with milk, then carry the lot to my room. She's still hidden under the quilt, so I put them on the floor.

Then I leave again, taking my novel to the couch, where I pretend to read chapter seven. I pretend for hours.

When Bec comes to check on me, I tell her I'm sorry, that I've got to get three chapters finished. She believes me and I feel guilty for lying.

I don't know what life is like for Mia. Not really. I don't know what's brought her here, of all places, when she has such a vocal, adoring fan club in Perth, a whole other world away.

I wait another ten minutes then go back, opening the door to a crumple of blankets and an empty cup and plate.

Mia's standing deep in my closet, rummaging through stored things: boxes of Legos, a signed football, an old stamp collection, two copies of *Playboy*. I don't cringe—they're from years ago when bodies were novelties.

"Can I help you?"

She turns, clutching magazines. "Helga."

"Zac. What are you doing?"

She sniffs as if for the last time. "I need money."

18
Mia

He offers me forty bucks from his second drawer, but I close my eyes and drive my fingers into my temples. I'm not in the mood for this.

"What? The jocks are clean," he laughs.

"It's not enough."

I don't have time for jokes. Beneath the quilt, I'd made a new Plan D: Albany, Adelaide, Sydney. I checked the bus times on my phone. The new Plan D needs money, not a stand-up fucking comedian.

"Have you got more?"

He points to a tea tin. "There's a year's worth of coins in there. It'll be heavy, though . . . Better yet, there could be some valuable stamps in that collection."

"Something else."

I scan the room, looking for anything of worth. There's so much crap in here—posters, trophies, a signed football, a globe, weights and a chin-up bar behind the door. The room stinks of

Axe and dirty socks. Why do guys' bedrooms always smell the same?

"What's this?"

He squeezes the metal thing in demonstration. "A wrist strengthener."

"Fuck, how strong do you want a wrist to be?"

He shrugs. "The PT said it was a good idea . . ."

In a corner there's a TV, a PlayStation 3, and a pile of games. Pinned to a corkboard is a booklet and a list of banned foods.

"They gave me one of those. Not as . . . extensive as yours, though. No pâté for twelve months? Helga, how do you cope?"

On the desk is a laptop, an iPod, and a messy pile of CDs. The top one has handwriting I recognize. *Lady Gaga for Rm 1.*

I pick it up and trace the blue pen with my finger. I remember writing it for him, though it feels like two lifetimes ago.

It was a strange request, I thought at the time. I could have given him the original CD, but I chose to hang on to it. I kept everything Rhys gave me. Instead, I copied the album and slipped it under his door. I didn't expect him to keep it.

I remember his knock on the wall that first day, as if he had something to tell me. I remember overhearing conversations with his mum, his voice more interesting and real than anyone else's in that hospital. And I remember how pale and sad he was when he didn't know I was watching.

I put the CD down. I haven't come all this way to reminisce.

"How much is in your bank account?"

"You're kidding."

"You think?"

"Shit, Mia, you can't . . . I mean . . . don't you . . ."

"What? Tick-tock."

He leans against the orange curtain and crosses his arms.

"I haven't seen you in three months. Okay, technically I never really *did* see you, except through the window. And now you turn up from nowhere, scare the flying crap out of me, and ask for money? It's not exactly . . . you know . . ."

"Not what?"

"Normal."

"Nothing's *normal* anymore, is it, Helga? For either of us. Besides, I'm not exactly robbing you. It's more like a loan."

"Why me?"

"Because you owe me."

"For what?"

"For lying."

"I didn't—"

I stomp my left crutch and it jars us both.

"You lied."

He looks at the rubber stopper pressed into the floor. "I didn't—"

"You told me I was . . . you said I was the luckiest on the ward."

He seems pale again. Is he swaying, or am I?

"You were."

I stamp the floor again.

"You *are*," he says quickly. "It's not my fault," he tells me, and he's right. None of this is his fault, but it's not mine either.

"You told me I should trust you."

He nods, remembering. He'd said that and more. He told me things I shouldn't have believed.

"I need a friend," I lie. "And about three hundred bucks to get to Sydney. My aunt Maree lives there—she's expecting me. I'll pay you back once I get there. I'll transfer it directly, with interest, if that's what you're worried about."

Arms folded, he takes his time. I think he's trying to read me, so I do my best to keep my face on straight. If I look away, he's got me.

"Mia, it's not the money I'm worried about."

I can't cry yet, not until after, when I'm on a bus out of here, then another, and another, where no one asks questions about my leg, where I'm going, or what I'm leaving behind. I need to go so far that I forget what I'm crying about.

So I fake a smile and laugh. "You don't have to worry about me, Zac." I use his name deliberately, and he smiles too. My heart's hammering so hard, he can probably hear it. He deserves better, I know, but I don't have a choice.

"You're a friend, Zac, a good friend. And I trust you. I'll pay you back, okay? I've organized this with my aunt. She's got a place you can see the harbor bridge from. It'll be sweet. Trust me."

His blue-gray eyes burrow into me, further than I want them to. I wonder what he sees.

Then he relaxes and nods.

Fuck, I think. *This is going to hurt us both.*

• • •

"Riding an . . . ATV is number . . . six . . . on my banned list," he shouts as the wheels find every hollowed ditch along the back driveway. The bike plunges and lurches and I've got to hold tight to the grips behind him. My crutches are pressed against his back. "The doctors say . . . it's too easy . . . to come off."

"So don't come off," I yell.

The bike bounces and I smack my chin on his shoulder. Blood's bitter in my mouth.

"Then don't wriggle," he says.

"I'm not wriggling."

We finally make it to the highway, where Zac pushes up through the gears. I hold on to my wig and lean forward. His hair whips at my lips.

"Why are you going so slow?" I shout.

"It's as fast as this one goes."

The ATV straddles the shoulder and the highway as cars roar by. We pass rows of trees to the right, then a cheese factory, a cidery, and a pear orchard. I'd come this way last night after walking from the hostel in the dark, but I hadn't noticed the signs. I'd been focusing on the gravel in front of me, taking one slow step at a time. I was zombie-tired and it took forever.

We pass a cricket field and a school, then take the turnoff for town. Zac doesn't go down the main street, but veers us around the back of a quiet parking lot.

He idles the engine, then turns it off. "You okay?"

I release my hands from the grips and shake them. "I'm alive."

"Mum would kill me . . ."

Backpack on, I make good speed with the crutches. I should—I've had enough practice. Zac has to jog to catch me.

"Were you always so fast?"

"Sportsgirl of the Year, Como Primary, two years running."

I was even faster when I reached high school, playing center for club volleyball until it eventually dawned on me that getting up early on Saturday mornings actually sucked. I soon learned there were better things to do with weekends.

"Were you always so slow?" I say, though I know better. I've seen his Facebook photos and old videos uploaded by his football team. I've seen him. He's fast.

Was fast. I have to remind myself we've both shifted tense.

"You're so slow, my gran could beat you," I say.

"I thought you said your gran died."

"Exactly."

The sight of the bank's logo cranks up my speed. The crutches dig at my armpits and my leg throbs, but I can't slow down now. I won't want to be mucking around with money or goodbyes when the bus pulls into town.

But the bank's doors don't slide open for me. I move toward the sensor, then away, but nothing.

"Fuck. Seriously?"

I pull my phone from my backpack to check the time. It's 8:50—too early for banks. I see there's a message from Shay.

> WTF? I cant believe u did that

And another from Mum.

> Mia, where the hell are you?

Delete. Delete. I chuck the phone back into my bag.

"So how'd you get here, then, without money?"

I cup my hands to peer through the glass. Where is everyone?

"The Greyhound. Perth to Adelaide."

"You've already got a ticket?"

I pull it out of my pocket and flash it at him.

"The driver stopped for a smoke at every bloody town, so I got off at this one for a Diet Coke from the machine. One of your petting farm brochures was there."

"In the Coke machine?"

"*Beside* the machine, in one of the tourist stands . . . Then the shuttle bus turned up and I thought, What the hell?"

"You came? I didn't see you."

"You weren't looking. I thought I could just get another bus, but the drivers are wankers. I'm seriously busting for a pee. Where *is* everybody?"

"At home, probably. It's Sunday."

I glare at him. He's right. Why didn't he say something earlier? Is he trying to mess with me?

"My brain's foggy," he says. "Not much sleep, for some reason . . . There's an ATM about a block away."

Goddamn, I really need to pee. I can't think straight.

"The restrooms are over there." Zac points to a cream-colored block. "Why don't you go, I'll get the cash, and I'll meet you back here in five, yeah?"

"Not just a pretty face, Zac."

He beams and it looks good on him, better than I could've

imagined. I appreciate it for a couple of seconds, hoping to re-member it.

"You better go."

"Yep, hold my bag," I say.

I make the mad sprint to the toilets. Even on crutches, I reckon I could still break school records.

19
Zac

I watch her go, *click creak, click creak, click creak.* Her blond wig sways with each swing of the crutches. I see how the left leg of her jeans hangs at an angle.

Then I duck behind the side of the bank, kneel on the cement — what choice do I have? — and dig through her backpack. There's a jumble of clothes and crap. There are bandages and pills. There's a purse with cash and a provisional driver's license showing how she used to look, with long hair, cherry lip-gloss, and a knock-'em-dead smile. It's the kind of beauty that catches people off-guard. It's a face you'd do anything to please. I want to please her, but not like this.

I search her cell. There's no Maree under *M*, or aunt under *A*. There have been no outgoing calls for ten days. There are some older texts, though, from her mum, wanting to know where she is. But no replies.

I don't want to be the latest dickhead in a long line of dickheads that she weaves through with her cherry lies. Whatever she's scheming, I'm not about to fund it.

I hear the *click creak* of her return, so I zip up the backpack and meet her halfway, near the butcher's.

"Relief." Mia laughs as she swings up the pavement. She flashes her full smile, and even with that cheap wig she can still pack a punch. With a face like hers, she must have spent her whole life getting what she wanted. It's not easy to resist.

"Sorry, I just get this bladder-brain condition sometimes. When my bladder's full, the brain kind of switches off, you know?"

"I've only got thirty bucks," I say, showing her my bank card as if it's proof. I hate the way it rips the smile from her. How tempting it is to give her all my savings in return for her perfect, fleeting thanks.

"I spent the rest. I forgot—sorry."

Mia doesn't react the way I expected. She doesn't stomp or swear or shout. She just folds into herself and closes her eyes.

"You can stay at my house tonight . . . or there's a hostel near here."

Mia turns and presses her forehead against the glass pane of the butcher shop.

"The hostel's not so bad," I say. "I don't mind paying, if it helps. It's only twenty bucks."

When she shakes her head, the wig shifts a little. She doesn't bother to fix it. "Twenty-five," she mumbles, though I barely hear it. It's like the glass has turned to sponge, soaking up her words. "Before I came to your house, that's where I was."

"Was it too loud?"

The answer's so small, I almost miss it. "I paid, but all they had were top bunks."

And there it is: the unspeakable thing.

Whatever's happened to Mia, it's emptied her. It's left behind a girl with fake hair, fake plans, and nowhere in the world she actually wants to be.

There's so much I don't know, but I do know she's not a bad person. Not really.

What would Dad do?

What would Mum do?

I do what someone should have done already. I hook my arms around her and pull her in, even though she tenses. I feel her struggle, the way an injured animal would, so I hold her tighter and feel her twist against me, again and again, wrenching and writhing, spitting muffled words into my T-shirt until something finally breaks and she sinks into me. I breathe her in.

Trust me, I think. *Trust me.*

Then she tilts into me like I'm the only friend left in the world.

• • •

I go even slower on the ride home. I have to keep looking over my shoulder to check that she's still there. Her left hand grips the handrail; her right holds down the wig. She has her eyes closed as if she's on a boat, bracing herself against the next wave.

I pass the cidery and orchards, and the turnoff for our farm. I ride past the end of our olive grove and keep on going, past Petersen's pistachios, then farther past the new estate and winery. Somewhere after rows of rippling vineyards, Mia slides her left arm around my waist.

There's no plan. All I want to do is follow this road for the rest of the day and probably all night, but the ATV has other ideas.

We roll to a stop near bushland.

The tank's bone dry. My brother's managed to screw this up for me.

"Not good?" Mia chews a fingernail, waiting for an answer.

I shake my head, more in disbelief than in reply. It's surreal to see her out here.

"It felt good, though, didn't it? For a while."

I sit beside her on the seat and nod. It felt awesome.

"What are you going to do?"

I shake my head and laugh. I'm in such deep shit right now, there's only one person who would know how to clear it.

20
Mia

I'm in his sister's living room, supposedly out of earshot. I hear enough.

"You can't *keep* her."

"I know—"

"She's not a stray dog."

"I *know*. It's not for long."

"What did her mum say?"

Zac lowers his voice. "They don't get on. Mia moved out after—"

"She's running *away*?"

"Maybe. I don't know."

"What the hell were you doing on an ATV? Mum would kill you."

"She doesn't need to know. Can you keep it a secret? All of it?"

A joey sniffs at the hem of my jeans. Each time I shoo it away, it comes right back. It's only small, but I don't trust its paws at my leg.

"I'm nearly out of firewood—"

"I'll get the ax."

"God, Mum would kill us both. Just go nick some from the olds."

Zac peers in at me from the hallway. He seems relieved I'm still here. "Bec needs wood. *Firewood,* I mean."

"I heard that!"

"She won't hurt you. The joey, I mean. Or Bec."

"I'm okay."

The door bangs shut behind him and I'm alone again in this room with too much wood already: the floorboards, television cabinet, coffee table, and clock. In the fireplace, wood crackles and snaps. The air stinks like smoke and wet fur.

I've never seen a real fire before. It's supposed to be relaxing, isn't it? But the flames burn my eyes and I have to look away. I have to get out of here.

Bec's pretty in a sun-bleached, unkempt way. Her long shock of wavy blond hair falls down the denim shirt that's stretched over her belly. She offers me a baby's bottle of milk.

"I'm fine, thank you."

"It's for the joey. I thought you might want to feed her."

I shake my head. Bec hoists the kangaroo into her arms and it sucks on the teat.

"What's broken?"

"Broken?"

"You're on crutches."

"I tore a ligament at volleyball. It's getting better."

In the fireplace, sparks shoot upward. If only a life could crackle and vanish so easily. If only I could turn to smoke and drift.

"Here's the thing: Zac's worried about you and I worry about Zac. That's kind of my job. He says you two are old friends. You are, aren't you?"

I nod, hoping it's enough.

"I've got two spare rooms, though one's got color samples on the walls. I'll be painting it for the baby."

"I just need—"

"Money for a bus, I know, but you shouldn't be crossing a continent on crutches. Your aunt will understand if you leave in a few days."

Fuck.

"I can't have Zac worrying, because then I'll worry, and that'll worry Junior here. Then he'll come out preemie and everyone will worry and we don't want that, do we? So stay until it's healed, okay?" She poses it like a question, though it isn't..

I nod and smile, but I'm leaving already in my mind. It's not Bec's fault. She doesn't know it's already too late.

"You want a hot drink? I don't have coffee, sorry. We're all tea-drinkers here."

The front door bangs and Zac comes in with a load of wood and a ridiculous grin. "Stealth! Mum didn't suspect a thing."

He feeds the fire carefully, as if there's a skill to it. I trust Zac. For what it's worth, I even trust his sister.

It's me I'm not so sure of.

• • •

I lock the bedroom door from the inside. I lock the window, too, and draw the curtains. Then I peel back the wig and push it under the pillow. I scratch at my scalp. My hair's growing back, but unlike Zac's, there's not enough. He's had five months since his last chemo. I've only had two.

My phone beeps twice.

Mia, ru getting these? Text me. Tell me where u are.

I hope Mum gives up soon. Everything she does makes this worse.

I set my alarm for four, then switch off the phone. I plan to get away in the dark, before Zac can find me. I'll make my own way to town and hole up somewhere, waiting for the bus. I'll use my ticket and go to Adelaide, like I planned. I've got to leave before kindness turns to meddling. I've already left one mother behind; I don't need a replacement.

I take the last two painkillers in the packet, then check the prescription refills in case I've misread the numbers.

I haven't.

Tomorrow's going to hurt. Better off on a bus, I think, taking the pain with me. It hurts less when I'm moving.

Bec's spare bed is soft when I lie in it. The blankets smell of mothballs, reminding me of Gran. I reach across to tap the base of the lamp once, twice, three times before it goes out. I sink deeper into the mattress, waiting for the drugs to soften what's left of the edges.

Four glow-in-the-dark stars seem to float from the ceiling. They're only plastic, so why do they shimmer and shift, as if real?

Each time I blink, the stars swirl and dissolve, skimming across my eyes like tears that should know better.

21
Zac

I'm sneaking the back way to Bec's house when I get sprung by Mum. Since when does she weed the pumpkins at eight a.m.?

"You're up early, Zac."

"Just making the most of the morning." I stretch like an eighty-year-old.

"How's *Pride and Prejudice*?"

Worse than a lumbar puncture. "Not so bad."

"Thought you'd be finished. Didn't see much of you yesterday."

Now that I'm on Mum's radar, I'll have to postpone my visit to Mia.

"Chapter eight and still nothing's happened."

Mum laughs. "We should rent the movie."

"We?"

"Well, the men will be picking and Bec wants to get painting. It'll be fun. I'll make popcorn."

Shit. The only thing worse than a suspicious mother is a bored one.

Even the movie is lost on me. Who cares about Keira Knightley and the guy from *Spooks*? How can I feign interest in gossiping socialites when Mia's only fifty meters away? That's if she hasn't done a runner and taken off. When I go for a leak, I phone Bec's number, but it rings out. Mia's cell diverts to voice mail.

She could be anywhere by now.

• • •

Bec's door won't open for me. I didn't even know it had a lock.

I follow the veranda around the front of the house. Through the living room window I see Bec on the couch with her feet up, her laptop balanced on the dome of her belly.

When I tap the glass, she looks up lazily. It takes her a few seconds to spot me, and when she does her reaction is audible.

"Fuck me!" She slides the laptop off and pushes up the window. "You shouldn't scare a woman in her third trimester."

"Why's the front door locked?"

"To keep out the drop bears."

"Do I look like a freaking drop bear?" I hear the whine in my voice.

"Haven't you got a novel to read?"

I see Anton, her partner, wave jerkily at me via Skype. I lean in through the window and wave back.

"Go home," Bec says.

"What's going on?"

"You're interrupting . . ."

"You know what I mean. Where's Mia?"

"She's busy. So am I."

"Bec!"

She angles the laptop screen away from us. "You told me to keep her a secret," she whispers.

"I didn't mean from *me!* Is she here?"

"I haven't eaten her; she's too skinny."

"Have you checked her room?"

"Not today."

"You have to. Mia's got, like, two alter egos: Hiding Mia and Houdini Mia. When she wants to go, it's just . . . *poof.*"

"The girl can barely walk. There is no *poof.*"

"She's faster than you think. Go check."

"Give her some space. Now rack off — you're wasting data." She pulls the window down, then blows me a kiss.

I leave, shocked. I'd confided in Bec because I thought she could help. I hadn't meant for her to take over.

Give her some space, she'd said. Does that mean Mia's still there?

Neither of them answers the phone. The front door stays locked all day, and I get the same response each time I knock: *Go read your book. Give her some space.*

It's only at night that I get any answers. Through the curtains of Bec's spare room, a low light glows. So she's there after all. She's okay.

J.R. keeps me company in the pumpkin bed, gently smacking me with his tail. We sit there until the light goes out, and then a while after that.

• • •

Bec hands me pink gloves and a bucket.

"Morning, sunshine."

"So?"

"So . . ."

I shove teats into kids' mouths. "Have you checked on Mia this morning?"

She shrugs, feigning innocence.

"Well, have you told Mum?"

Bec grins over the sucking of the kids. "Our mother doesn't need to know everything."

And neither do I, apparently, as she ignores the rest of my questions through the day. An impenetrable force field has descended over her house, and when I tap at the kitchen window in the afternoon, Bec shoos me away, saying that Mia is sleeping.

"At four?"

"She sleeps a lot," Bec whispers, as if talking about a baby. "She must need it."

I creep around to the spare room. I don't knock at the window. Instead, I slip a note between the glass and the frame.

> *Hey neighbor*
> *Do you need anything? If Bec's cooking is dodgy, I can bring you a grilled cheese, ok?*
> *Or a hot chocolate. Whatever you want.*
> *If Bec's holding you hostage for slave labor, just call and I'll bust you out. I'm not far away.*
> *Zac*

It's been two days. Why won't she answer?

• • •

The silence is seriously fucking with me.

I spend the next two days in the shed, trying to occupy myself with the crib pieces. I saw and sand. My sanity's slipping away. What's with all the secrecy?

On the fifth day, I lose the plot. I chuck the tools and storm out to Bec's house, ready to force entry if I have to.

But Bec's on the front veranda, soaking her hand in Dettol.

"The bitch bit me."

"Bit you?"

"Don't go near her; she's crazy."

"What happened?"

"I was just checking her for ticks."

"Mia?"

"*Daisy* bit me. Your stupid alpaca."

I'm so confused. Bec tuts. "And I thought you were Mia's friend . . ."

It's the final straw. "So did I! Bec, you're taking the piss. It's been five fucking days."

"Calm down, Zac."

"Calm down? I'm worried sick. She's probably fucked off to the other side of the country."

"She hasn't. She's here—"

"How would you know? You don't even know that. Mia!" I shout.

"Shhh. She's in the bath. Zac, don't—" Bec grabs my arm but I yank it free and rush around the outside of the house. I knock on the bathroom louvers, but the sound is dull, so I call her name.

"Mia."

I tilt the louvers a bit more.

"Mia?"

"I'm here," a small voice answers. There's a slosh of water. It's her.

I close my eyes and rest my palms against the louvers. The glass is lumpy and cool.

"Just tell me you're okay."

"I'm okay."

I feel like an idiot, but now I know. She might be hiding, but at least she's not fighting or running.

And it's more than I could've hoped for.

22
Mia

I've never been in a real bathtub. This one stands alone, wide and deep and stained. The enamel is cool and smooth. The warm water comes almost to the top.

In this bathtub, water is sud-slippery. It fills each space without judgment. Nothing hurts.

Hours pass. There's nothing to tell how slowly. I've let my phone go dead, paranoid someone would track me.

Sounds skim under the door. There's the close cheeping of chickens. Farther out, grunts and bleats merge into a soundtrack that's already become ordinary.

I used to hate spending time alone; now it's all I crave. In the hospital, too many people came prying. What would *they* know? I hated every one of them.

But not as much as I hated my mother. How is it that at seventeen I'm old enough to drive, have sex, and get married, but not old enough to decide what happens to my body? Given the choice, I'd rather have died than let them do what they did.

But I didn't get that choice. My mother signed the form

while I was on the operating table, the tumor holding tight to the artery it had wrapped itself around. "We had to act immediately," surgeons told me later. "An excision and bone graft were no longer practicable." Consent was needed. They didn't wake me up; they handed my mother a pen. She signed her name and ruined my life.

Did they use a power saw?

I slide down and go under, letting the back of my head bump against the bottom. Water slips and slops above. Down here, I hear my heart resound through water. Its two-part rhythm is low and willful in my ears. It surprises me how insistent it sounds, even after all of this.

"Mia."

It reaches me like a memory. I lift myself and check the door is locked. It is. My crutches lean against it. The voice comes floating through the window.

"I'm okay," I tell Zac, though I'm not. I'm not okay. I'm tired. I'm hurting.

I don't have energy for Zac. I don't have energy for anything. All I can manage is to make the daily journey from my bedroom to the bathroom in Bec's long robe. I'm more tired than ever. How can Zac get up and feed the animals, cracking jokes like the world is exactly how it should be? Perhaps for him it is. He might have someone else's marrow, but at least he's got two legs.

Fuck. I reel again. After all this time, it still catches me off-guard. I sink underwater once more. How long does it take for the brain to catch up? Each morning I open my eyes to the same sickening shock.

I have to remember not to look down. I have to clip the

thing on and get dressed quickly, hiding the temporary prosthetic that rubs my wound till it bleeds. It burns like hell, but I have to keep it on, keep it hidden, unclipping it only for the bath or bed. In water, at least, the scars don't hurt so much.

Such a pretty word: *scar.*

The ugliest is *stump.* I woke to a stump. The surgeons congratulated one another for saving the knee and a part of the shin. They boasted, over and over, that I was lucky.

Lucky?

While my friends were dancing at Summadayze, I was kept in observation with intravenous morphine. I pitched in and out of the world, visited by shrinks who attempted to talk about change and perspective and body image and luck. Then they hooked me to more chemo. I couldn't eat, wouldn't talk, didn't watch when the wound was unbandaged or the staples taken out. I tried to trick myself beyond my fucked-up body, slipping between vivid dreams until the morphine was taken away and I was left to live like this.

Against my will, I resurface. My head falls against the side of the tub. At this angle, I see every beam of the ceiling. Sixteen of them. At this angle, I don't have to see myself. My body can be perfect. It can be anything I imagine it to be.

So I stay in the bath for hours, hearing the animals and the floorboards that creak beneath Bec's weight. In this house, wood flexes and yields. Even the walls, somehow, seem to bend for the people within. I've never known a house to be soft. Bec, too, is unexpectedly kind. Yesterday, she asked for my opinion on paint swatches. "A new coat of paint for a new soul," she said, levering open a tub of olive green.

Bec hums as she paints. Through the day, she brings me

sandwiches and sliced pears and expects nothing in return but the safekeeping of her brother.

She can relax: I didn't come here to hurt Zac. I don't want their money, either, anymore. I've got enough to get to Adelaide, at least. Enough to get out of here.

I have to start again or not at all.

23
Zac

Thump, pat, pause. Thump, pat, pause.

The sequence comes from inside Bec's house. It reminds me of Mia on her crutches. But isn't she still in the bath?

I go around the back of the house, passing the baby's room with its windows opened to release the stink of paint. Outside the spare room, I stop and listen.

Thump, pat, pause. Thump, pat, pause.

There's a gap between window and frame, so I draw the curtain to one side. I recognize the end of a brown tail. It thumps the floor, then slides from view.

"Get out of there," I whisper, opening the window some more. I lean in, trying to coax the joey to me. "Come here."

She doesn't come, so I pull myself through the window. Inside, I crouch and click my fingers at the joey, now sniffing the spilled contents of Mia's backpack: a jumble of clothes, a tube of gel, a phone.

"Come—"

It's not the mess of Mia's life that stops me. It's not the empty packets of pills.

It's the half-leg in the corner of the room. It starts with a flesh-colored socket, like an oversize champagne flute. It tapers down to a pole with screws and a harness. Beneath is a stripy sock that ends in a blue shoe, its laces tied in a perfect white bow.

It knocks me with unexpected force. Mia. The hollow socket. The chunky clasp. The neat white bow that shouldn't be.

A hand at my back shocks me. Bec slides her other arm around her belly, like she's shielding her baby from all the harm that could ever happen.

I gasp for breath and Bec tightens her grip around all three of us, drawing us together.

"I know," she says. "I know."

We shut the door to the bedroom and release the joey outside. It springs indifferently away. Goats bleat and the sky is too bright, too blue for this.

"I think, perhaps . . ." begins Bec. "I think she needs her mum."

• • •

I sit in the cool shed, grateful for solitude. Laid out around me are the wooden slats and plans for the crib. There's no urgency to finish this: the baby's another six weeks away at least.

With a chisel, I dig into the flesh of a post head. Thin spirals peel away. My incisions become vines that curl around, twisting and tangling the length of it. I carve tiny leaves. In each leaf, I etch veins. I zoom in on every detail, though I'm wasting my time. Nothing I do could ever make her better. Nothing I say would make it right. This chisel, this hammer, these nails—they're useless. Mia's not tough enough for this. For *that*. The ugly leg. All this time I'd suspected, but never known for sure. I'd watched her lying to strangers. *Tore a ligament at volleyball*, she'd say in that offhand way. She had a way of making you believe. I wanted to believe her, and I did, for a while. I watched those cherry lips and I swallowed those lies. I wanted to believe that she'd be okay, that an exciting future was only a bus trip away. But it's not. It's not okay.

"I haven't seen much of Bec lately."

It's Mum, by the entrance. When did it get so dark outside?

"Have you?" she asks.

"She reckons her legs have puffed up. *Cankles*, or something."

"Should I help you clear the poo, then?"

"What?"

"It's Friday, Zac."

I release the chisel and it rolls along the bench. "No. I'll ask Bec."

Her front door's locked, as expected, but I don't knock. I don't want to break the spell of this house anymore. I wait a few seconds, then turn away to leave.

Then, "No!" shouts a voice from inside.

I stop. *No?* Was it Bec? Was she calling me?

"Don't!"

It *is* Bec. I've never known my sister to be afraid of anything.

I push an ear to the door, hearing the "Farrrck!" that manages to rattle the entire house. "Faaarrrking hell!"

Fuck! Bec? Mia! I should have known—something had to give eventually.

I sprint around the house and yank open bathroom louvers, but they're too small to crawl through. Inside, Bec's voice is rising in anger. "Don't you *dare!*"

I target Bec's bedroom and force up her window. Panic escalates as I roll in, pick myself up, and dash to the kitchen, the epicenter of noise—"Fuck! Shit! Fuck! Shit!"—where screams amplify at the sight of me sliding in with golf clubs. I grab hold of the sink to slow my skidding. Then I hold on longer so I can take it all in.

I'd expected to see women engaged in combat, not this: Bec lying belly-up on the kitchen table like a beached whale beneath a bath towel. Mia bent over, her face buried in her hands.

"Zac!" Bec pants, clearly hysterical. "Oh my god, *Zac!*"

What the hell? "Is the baby coming?"

"God, I wish."

"What's happening?"

"Just do it. Quick!"

"What?" I yell.

Mia whips her hands from her face, reaches for Bec's knee, then rips a strip violently free. Bec bucks as if she's taken 3,000 volts from an electric fence and howls every swear word she's ever taught me and more.

The two golf clubs clatter to the floor.

"What the . . ."

Bec's a writhing, flailing buffalo with a four-letter-word

vocabulary. Tears stream down her face, which is twisted with pain. And . . . laughter?

"She said it wouldn't hurt!"

"It?"

She groans in a primeval way, then lets her head flop sideways to face me. "I'm trying to impress Anton. We haven't even *started* on the bikini line."

Beside her, Mia inhales into cupped hands—gulping, laughing—and it's the most awesome thing I've ever seen.

"Who does this? Please tell me labor is less painful."

"Toughen up," I say, though I've never been more grateful to my sister.

"Oh, she's cruel. There's a whole tub of wax just sitting there." Bec shakes her head at me. "Oh, Zac. Oh shit, this is bad."

"Have you inhaled too many paint fumes?"

"Oh, Zac, you have no idea. We're really in the shit now."

I laugh. "We? I'm not the one covered in hot wax."

"So what's the joke?" Mum demands from the doorway. "Besides me?"

• • •

"You can't keep her—"

"I know."

"She's not an animal—"

"Mum, you sound like Bec."

"Well? Why didn't someone tell me?"

Bec and I exchange a look.

"What about her checkups and blood tests? Is she up to date?"

"She's not an animal," reminds Bec. "She did my eyes. Lashes and brows. Good, huh? I'd bypass the leg wax, though."

Mum sighs. "Don't be flippant. Someone's got to tell her mother."

24
Mia

I seek out the dark. It was always going to end like this: *Who's going to take care of her? Who's going to be sensible?*

Pins and needles stab my foot, though it's no longer there. Phantom pain—the cruelest fucking joke. They say cancer makes you stronger. It doesn't. It messes with your head. It gives you an itch you can't scratch and a heart that won't stop aching.

I have to go, but where? Not to friends with sly looks, or a mother who betrayed me. Not to doctors with power saws and lies. What else would they want to cut off?

Shit, it wasn't Plan D that brought me here. Plan D had played out weeks ago.

Coming here was Plan Z. Zac *was* the last chance. Even though we'd never met, he'd been more real than anyone in the hospital. That strange, pale boy with the knock became the only one with the right things to say.

"You know how chickens sort out their pecking order?" Zac wraps his arms over the fence beside me.

"No."

"That's what Mum and Bec are doing in there."

"Sorry. I'll go tomorrow."

"Home?"

I shake my head. Mum allowed this to happen. A goat nuzzles me, so I dip my hand in a tub of food and offer it my palm. Its tongue is dry and rough.

"Where?"

I shrug. It doesn't matter. "I keep thinking that if I get on a bus and go far enough, I'll eventually fall off the edge of the world."

"I hate to tell you this but . . ." Zac mimes a sphere with his hands.

"Spoilsport. I just want to disappear."

"You didn't go through chemo to disappear."

"Remember how angry I was about losing my hair? I thought *that* was a tragedy. At least hair grows back . . ."

"You fought, though." He says it like it's something to be proud of.

"I just wanted to be normal."

"You were . . ." he says. "You *are* . . ."

Poor Zac, still tripping over tenses. He must know about my leg. He should realize the word *normal* belongs to the past.

"If I'm so normal, why is everyone handing me brochures on wheelchair fucking basketball? I never liked basketball before, but now that I'm a cripple—"

"You're not."

I chuck the rest of the feed. "I'm a freak show."

"Mia, you don't know—"

"You *don't* know, Zac—"

"No, *you* don't know how beautiful you are."

The word topples me a little. *Beautiful?* I close my eyes. The earth feels like it's pitching beneath me.

"You are, Mia. You were and you are, and you always will be."

"Don't." I use the fence to steady myself. He's warping the night with lies.

"If you were at my school, I wouldn't talk to you. Couldn't. Look at you — you're gorgeous. Even with that blond wig, you're still hotter than any girls I know. You're a nine out of ten."

"I'm a number now?"

"On the universal hierarchy of hotness, you'd easily be a nine. And I'd be like a six-point-five."

"You're a knob," I tell him, opening my eyes to catch his grin.

"Okay, so I'm probably more like a six. And sixes don't talk to nines — that's the rules."

"You're not a six, Zac. And I'm definitely not a nine."

"You know, there was only one thing stopping me from giving you a ten."

"Gee, I wonder . . ."

"And it's because you're a moody cow."

I punch him. He mouths an *ow*, rubbing his shoulder.

"That'll bruise."

"If your stupid hierarchy exists, Zac — and it doesn't — the truth is, you'd be way higher up than me. You're the normal one now."

"You want to make a bet?"

"Sure." It's a competition I can't lose. With a crutch, I tap both of his boots. *One, two.*

"Yeah, but what about everything else? I'm stuck here, repeating year twelve, while my mates have gotten on with their lives. I'm taking eleven pills a day, getting platelets counted each week. I can't do anything half interesting. I'm even banned from picking olives, for god's sake. This isn't real life, it's limbo."

"At least you *look* normal. People don't stare—"

"I'm only a fifty-five." Fifty-five? What scale is he using now? That's when I notice how tightly he's clenching the wire. Tendons lock over knuckles. Muscles flex in his forearms.

"Zac, I don't get it. What's a fifty-five?"

But he hooks a foot on a rung and hoists himself onto the fence, above me. A chill creeps through my body and I wonder if it reaches him too. He shivers.

"Zac?"

"Fifty-five percent. My chance of living five years without relapse."

I've never been good with numbers, never needed to be. But I understand this one. Fifty-five falls cleanly into my head the way a coin chinks into a money box. Numbers are what they are. They can't be argued with.

Everything else melts away except for a cold number and a boy who's looking to the stars as if he knows them.

"Zac, you can't know that."

"Google it."

I'd assumed that after leaving the hospital he'd stopped obsessing over statistics. I didn't think numbers had followed him all the way down here. Maybe numbers torment him the way my leg torments me. Maybe we're both only living as fractions.

Fifty-five is a pass, I think. A fifty-five percent in Math

—171

or English would be good enough for me. Should I tell him it's good enough?

"Mia, you'll be a ninety-eight by now."

Well, I'd rather be a fifty-five with two legs than a ninety-eight with one, I decide, as if this could trump him, but the wind steals the words from my lips and tosses them away. I'm glad they're gone.

And still he looks up, where thousands of stars fill the arc of the sky. Of all that's random and uncertain in the universe, how can a boy be so sure of a single number?

"You've got the rest of your life to be angry, Mia. Me . . . I don't know what I've got."

"Did you see that?" I point, desperate to bring him back. "A shooting star."

"A burning meteorite."

"So I can't make a wish?"

He shrugs. "If you want to make a wish on a burning meteorite, then make a wish."

I punch his thigh. "Spoilsport. Help me up."

Zac braces me as I put my good foot on a wire and, pulling at him, swing the other leg up and over. I straddle the fence, facing him, not trusting myself to balance the way he does. Beneath my jeans, blood rushes my scar, making the wound throb. My head's dizzy but it's worth it to be level with him. I notice the gray in his eyes. The squareness of his jaw.

"Hey, you were supposed to be cheering *me* up, remember?"

"Was I?"

"It's in your job description. We can't both be miserable—it doesn't work like that." I snap my fingers. "So stay focused."

"I'll try. Where was I?"

"You were about to say bon voyage for my bus trip. And I was going to promise to send you a postcard . . ." I nudge him playfully. Then I slap his chest for real. "Come with me!"

"What?"

"Why not? You and me and a Greyhound." The idea soars. The freedom of it.

"Where?"

"Don't wreck it with details—just come."

"You're serious?"

I nod, but he laughs and looks away.

"Shit, Mia, I can't take off—"

"You can."

"I've got year twelve, and Mum. And the others. After all they've been through—"

"They'd understand."

"They need me here, on the farm. They need me . . . well."

I need you too, I think, but I keep my lips closed, just in case.

Zac slides a hand over mine, linking his fingers through. I hadn't imagined how warm his skin would be, or how much I'd been waiting for his touch. His hand calms me. It stops the throb of my leg. It fixes the stars.

When he speaks, he picks his words carefully. "I know you don't believe me, Mia, but you *are* lucky. I'd swap places with you if I could."

I flinch. It's not possible. "You wouldn't."

"If I could promise my parents a ninety-eight, I would."

"I'd swap too," I counter, but he squeezes my hand until it hurts.

Zac's mum shouts our names, calling us in, but neither of us moves. Balanced on the fence, with our fingers locked around each other's, it's all we can do to hold ourselves in place.

• • •

Later, after the cold of night has reached our bones, we untangle. This time, I follow Zac to his house. I'm quiet on my crutches beside him. An alpaca grunts as we pass.

Zac helps me through the window, then pulls the curtains behind us, shutting out the universe.

When I crawl into Zac's bed, I don't unclip the prosthetic. I keep my jeans on, and so does he. We both stink of feed and dirt, and soon the sheets do too. I curl and he curls behind me, denim against denim.

Tonight, I want to forget myself. I want to be in someone's arms, safe from nightmares: not dreaming, sleeping. I want to be more than a fraction.

In the darkness, our arms and legs coil to make a whole.

25
Zac

I wake to feel Mia in the arc of me, her chest rising and falling, her wig splayed on the pillow.

It's three a.m. I know that around the world, 1,484 people will be diagnosed with cancer this hour. Almost twenty-five this minute.

But what are the odds of this? Shared breath, soft flesh, and the staggering possibility that life can be good again.

• • •

Light floats in as specks, looking for skin to land on. There's a haze of warm air and heavy quilt.

"I hate to inform you," I mumble, "but you've been downgraded to an eight."

"Hmm?"

"For snoring."

"Crap. On the plus side, you've been upgraded to a seven."

"Seven?"

"Good arms," she tells me.

We coast in and out of consciousness until there's a knocking at my door. Mia stiffens.

It's Bec's voice calling. "Zac, she's gone. But her stuff's still in the room."

"Then she'll be back."

We stay, even when our stomachs grumble and daylight pierces the curtains.

"Correction," I say. "You're back up to a nine."

Mia crinkles her brow, unaware of how I'm seeing her now: no blond wig, just a sheen of short brown hair that frames her small face. With a finger, I trace a curl near her ear.

"It's Emma Watson, post *Harry Potter*. Why the hell have you kept this from me?"

Mia burrows beneath a pillow but I find her there.

She groans. "It's too short."

"Have you *seen* Emma Watson?"

"Not as much as you, obviously . . ."

"It's hot."

"Then why only a nine?"

"You're still a moody cow."

"Shut up and tell me a story. I want to fall back to sleep."

Under the quilt, I tell her about the baby's crib, still in pieces. I describe the last lot of backpackers and Evan's attempts to woo a Frenchie. I tell her how a year ago a Dutch worker ate a whole cooked chicken from the local deli and ended up with food poisoning, crapping under every fifth olive tree, from one end of the farm to the other.

"Then Bec gave Anton Gastro-Stop and a spare room and, for some inexplicable reason, fell in love with him."

"Where is he now?"

"Up north for another fortnight. Bec told him to get the bug out of his system before the baby. The travel bug, I mean. He didn't want to, but she usually gets her way."

"Is he nice?"

"Yeah, though we still give him shit . . . about the shits. He says the weirdest stuff. Like, if something's easy, he'll say, *Little apple, little egg.*"

Mia sounds it out. "What else?"

When she smiles, I realize that Mia doesn't need to cross Australia—she just needs an escape from herself for a bit. So I tell her everything that comes into my head: how Johnno Senior left a sheep for each of us kids in his will, and how this led to a goat and two alpacas.

"People were coming to buy oil, but they were staying to pat the animals. Dad was stoked, and the petting farm kind of grew out of that. It made me popular, as a kid. *More* popular, I mean."

"What were you like, in primary school?"

"Not as good-looking, obviously. Obsessed with becoming handball champion of the world."

"And were you?"

I open my eyes to check if hers are still closed. They are. Her lips are parted and I notice the small gap between her front teeth.

"Of course. Weren't you?"

"I was hopscotch champion for a while. Tell me more."

I tell her the strange requests we've had for oils, like lobster- and chocolate-infused. And I tell her about Macka, my cricket coach, and how he chucked a tantrum when his giant pumpkin imploded two hours before the judging at the Albany show.

"Did you know that pigs have the same intelligence as four-year-old children?"

It's Mum's voice that snaps us out of it. "Zac, are you okay in there?"

"Yeah. Just reading chapter nine."

"Well, bring it with you. Your appointment's in twenty minutes so we'll need to leave in ten."

Mia throws back the quilt and I'm too slow to stop her when she calls, "That's okay, Mrs. Meier, I'll go with him. Little apple, little egg."

26
Mia

The receptionist notices my crutches and mistakes me for a patient.

"I'm here with Zac."

"Oh. Where's Wendy today?"

I shrug and flick through magazine articles on celebrities who are pregnant, heartbroken, fat, or anorexic. It was stressful enough just to enter this building, so there's no way I was going to follow Zac into that room. I don't need a doctor sniffing around. I know exactly what's wrong.

When he's done, I go with Zac to pathology but I wait outside while he gets his blood taken. I pull my cell from my pocket. I should be using this chance to call the bus company and book my ticket east. I have to go—I *want* to go—so why can't I make myself dial the number? There's nothing stopping me from getting on a bus today.

Nothing except a small, childish voice that asks, *What about last night?*

Being cocooned with Zac was the nicest thing that's happened for a long, long time. But how do I know if it meant anything, or if it was just convenience? A warm body on a cold night?

I dial the number and wait for the automated options. "Press one for new bookings, two for arrival times, three for timetables. Hold the line for other inquiries."

I hold the line, but when a woman answers, I hang up.

What about last night? What about it?

Then Zac bounds out of pathology and leads me across the street. He's talking nonstop about the pathologist's bad breath, and how she couldn't find a good vein. "They've got names, you know. Today we had to bring out Chuck Norris."

"Weird."

If Zac's wondering about last night, he doesn't show it. To be honest, he doesn't appear to be thinking much at all.

In the pharmacy, as we wait for his prescriptions to be made up, Zac raids the sunglasses stand. I watch him, waiting for a clue. *What about last night, Zac?* Why doesn't he say anything useful?

"What do you think?" He models a pair of oversize black glasses.

"They're ugly," I tell him, because they are. He looks like a fly.

"These too?" The rims are fluorescent yellow with huge stars. "Only two bucks. You could get the pink ones to match."

"Really."

"Hey, what if I buy a tube of this stuff for Evan? I could plant it in his room in case he brings a backpacker home. What would the French word for *hemorrhoid* be?"

"*Le hemorrhoid?*"

Zac laughs, then proceeds to try out every single tester of aftershave. That's when I'm reminded he's just Zac: harmless, naive Zac. He's just a boy with good arms. Whatever last night was, it wasn't real. Real life is a metal leg and an infection that keeps getting worse.

So I swing over to the makeup section and dial the bus company. I hold the line, unnerved by the blond girl reflected in rectangular mirrors. None of this is real. I tell the woman's voice my details. Today is full, but she confirms my seat for tomorrow. Then I slide the phone back into my pocket.

I used to spend hours in pharmacies like this. As a girl, I'd pick through lipsticks, eye shadows, and powders. I was mesmerized by the endless possibilities of body butters, fake tans, and pedicure packs.

These days I've got a one-track mind, so I turn toward the only thing that appeals: the rows of prescription painkillers behind the counter. I've raided Bec's cupboards, but I'll need something stronger for the ride. Before things turn ugly.

When Zac pays for his lot, I lean over and request the strongest over-the-counter drugs they have—"for my torn ligament," I tell the girl. When we're back in the pickup, I rip open the packet.

Zac takes off the yellow sunglasses. "Wait. You need food with those."

"I don't."

"You do. Hang on, there's a place I know. . ."

The pills grow sticky in my palm as Zac drives us out of town and down a bumpy turnoff to a semi-filled parking lot. He leads me inside the Contented Cow Company, where he pushes us through a handful of tourists, arms himself with toothpicks, and then, ninja-like, impales various cheese cubes at random.

"Analgesics and cheddar shish kebabs. What more could you want? Except for maybe a honey mead chaser." He passes me a plastic cup, then clinks the rims, as if it's a toast.

"Classy." I swallow the drugs. I know they won't take the pain away, but they'll help for a while. I lick the sweet liquid from my lips. It's good.

"Free cheese. Free honey mead. Seriously, you city folk have no idea what you're missing."

"Seriously, I think I might . . . I'm going, you know."

"Now?"

"Tomorrow. I booked my ticket."

"So we've got today." He checks his watch. "And I'm morally obliged, you realize, to show you exactly what you've been missing."

"Surely nothing can compete with the Contented Cow?"

He chucks the toothpicks and takes my hand. "Don't peak too soon. Come on."

• • •

For what's left of the afternoon, Zac drives us down every rutted turnoff that promises cheese, wine, beer, nuts, cider, or chutney. When we're standing at each counter, we become like every other tourist, faking organic preferences and gourmet tastes. I drain each cider and wine glass offered to me, but as designated driver, Zac spits into a bowl. I learn more than I ever thought possible about dukkah—a word I'd previously imagined was made up—blue cheeses, and quince paste. Soon, my stomach is churning with a *veritable mélange* of flavors. For now, my pain is forgotten. Thoughts bubble and fizz like sparkling wine.

Zac's phone rings, and for the third time he lets it go to voice mail.

"I know what you're doing, Zac."

"Being an excellent host and tour guide?"

"Apart from getting me drunk, you're avoiding going home to your mum."

"As if. Want some fudge?"

I cringe, pushing my fingers against my stomach. "God, no."

"There's a place . . ."

Zac drives us through new suburbs that skirt the coast, then across an empty block to a lookout over a rocky harbor. Small birds swing above the choppy ocean, swooping in sea spray.

There's no fudge. There's nothing around but us. When Zac switches off the engine, it occurs to me that this afternoon has all been about getting me here. He'd chosen this, the perfect spot, away from crowds and family, and the realization sobers me. I smooth my tongue across my teeth and comb my fingers through the wig. Perhaps last night meant something to him after all. Perhaps . . .

Zac drums the steering wheel and admires the swell through his star-shaped sunglasses. "What do you think?"

"It's . . . pretty." Why the hell am I so nervous?

"You know how to use a rod, don't you?"

A rod?

"I've got a six-foot, but there's a four-foot that's easier to handle."

Never in my life have I parked at a lookout with a guy who suggests fishing. Ever.

"I don't think . . ."

"I'll check in the back. There could be a hand line."

"No."

I don't want to fish. I hate the smell of bait, and besides, those rocks would take some scrambling over. I want to head back—now. My leg is sore, but worse, my face burns hot and I'd hate for him to notice.

I can't believe what a dick I've been. "It's too rough," I say.

"Not for the fish. We could get a dozen herring on a day like this. Come on, it'll be fun."

"Not for the fish."

He laughs.

"I'm going tomorrow," I remind him.

Zac pushes the glasses up onto his head. His eyes look more blue than gray. If he would kiss me now, I might believe some of the things he said last night: that I'm a nine out of ten; that I'm beautiful, still. If he would push me against the seat and grab at me, and want me, I'd know for sure.

But he doesn't. He just pulls the stupid glasses back into place and starts the engine.

I'm a complete idiot. All the compliments in the world mean nothing if he doesn't want to act on them.

Zac is just a nice guy trying to make me feel better.

And I'm a fucking fool for believing him.

• • •

I top up the bath, keeping it hot so my whole body scalds rather than just the one part.

In the living room, Bec's Skyping Anton. I hear them laugh at the way her belly jolts with surprising kicks. I hear in his voice how he misses her.

Blood has tinged the bath water pink. During chemo, I'd taken the pill to stop my cycles—nurses said I'd need all the blood I had. My period hadn't come back until tonight, a shock of dark red, mistakenly believing my body's okay again. If only it knew.

I run a hand between my hip bones where my belly dips. Menstruation is wasted on me. I'll never grow round like Bec, because no one will ever want to have sex with what's left of me. No one could ever love this.

My whole life, I've only ever been the pretty one—it's all I needed to be. But what am I now, without a leg? Without hair? Without the cool group at school to hang out with? Who could look at me with anything but disgust? Zac's the most decent guy I know, and even he's not attracted to me.

Without my looks, what's left? I'm not smart, or kind, or talented, or creative, or funny or brave. I'm nothing.

The bath turns cold. My fingers are crinkled when I lift myself up. I use the sink to help me hop out of the tub. A single wet footprint on the floor. I draw Bec's robe around me and steal some tampons from her top drawer. I put one in, then swing on crutches down the hall to my room, where I close the door behind me. I sit on the bed to pull on undies, then hop across to grab a shirt.

The knock is too quick. He's inside too soon, without thinking or waiting. It's too late for me to hide and too late for him to hide the shock that looks like repulsion as he turns to the wall and I'm screaming and hiding my chest, as if that matters; as if that's what could disgust him. He's saying *I'm sorry I'm sorry it's okay I'm sorry*, but it's not because he saw me and I saw his face and I can't stop screaming even when he kicks the robe toward me and I hold it over myself. He shuffles to me, hands in front, saying *it's okay it's okay it's okay it's okay* and I'm screaming at him not to come any closer. I want to jump out of the window and sprint for my life but I can't so I'm trapped and he's close, too close, so I punch him.

"You don't *do* that. You don't walk *in*—"

"I'm sorry."

"You can't look at it. Can't look at me—"

"It's okay."

"It's *not!* I hate you."

I push him so hard, he falls against the closet. Coat hangers jangle inside and he says, "Don't hate me."

"I hate you and this place and Bec, and your mum, and everyone acting like they're so fucking caring and normal, and it's all a huge lie. I hate you and you hate me—"

"I don't hate you."

"You think I'm ugly—"

"I don't—"

"Well, you should have a look at yourself."

He exhales like it hurts. "You're a nine."

"Then why don't you want to fuck me?"

"What? No . . . not like this." I pull the lamp from its socket and throw it at him. He doesn't step away, just lets it smash at his shoulder. He lets me hurt him. Then he picks up each of the pieces and leaves.

In the hallway, Bec fusses over him. "It's my fault," he tells her. "I went in. I wanted to tell her about Sheba's baby."

I hate him.

Bec knocks later, quietly.

"Mia."

I don't answer. The door's locked—I've learned my lesson. I sit on the floor thinking of ways to hurt myself.

"One of the alpacas gave birth tonight. It's a girl. You wanna come see?"

I hate them all.

27
Zac

I come out early to see the baby alpaca in the pen. Her wool is fluffy like a chicken's. Ten hours old, she can already stand on wonky legs.

When I check the other animals, I find a dead rooster. It was old. I open the coop and lift it out, then walk the path to the far fence, where I throw the body deep into the bush. I don't wait for the vixen today, though I know she'll be close.

"Stay away," I call over my shoulder, as if a deal could be made with a fox. *Have the bird but stay away from the new-born.* I fool myself into thinking killers have a conscience.

Some might.

But not all.

Some don't care about age or decency. Some come in daylight on a Saturday morning and snatch a grown man on his way home from the beach, sand on his soles, salt on the surfboard in the back of his pickup. A man with a C-shaped scar on the side of his head. *C for Cam. In case you forget.*

I'm in the shed brushing lacquer onto timber when Mum tells me. Dad and Evan are out loading the trailer.

"It was Nina who called. She thought you'd want to know. It was quick."

I scratch at a patch of dried varnish on my palm. I'm not sure I hear Mum right.

"You know Cam didn't have . . . good odds."

Yeah, but still. It wasn't supposed to happen yet. It was supposed to be drawn out for another twelve months, with more radiation and surgery, more scans and always a pocket of hope. Not a sudden heart attack—*major organ failure*—three kilometers from home. Did he get the chance to brake? Pull over? Was he aware of the song that was playing on the radio?

"At least he got a last surf in." I'm dizzy with the fumes.

"He always liked you." Mum squeezes my shoulders and I flinch. "What's wrong?" She finds the fresh bruise, and shakes at the touch. "Zac!"

"Don't stress, it was an accident."

"What happened?"

"Will there be a funeral?"

"Nina said there's a service tomorrow."

"In Perth?"

"Scarborough Beach. Are you sure you're all right?"

"I'll go."

"Good," Mum says, already making plans. "We can stay with Trish."

I notice a brush bristle stuck in a slat. I pull it out like a splinter.

"I'll take Mia."

"But isn't she going to—"

"No."

It's not the raw wound of her leg that haunts me. It's the expression on her face. She said she hated me but it wasn't hate I saw. It was terror.

I'm not scared of her; I'm scared *for* her. I'm scared of all the things she might do. I know she's going to run. She'll run from anyone who cares enough.

I care enough.

Cam died yesterday and there was nothing I could do about it. But Mia . . .

"I'm going to take her home."

• • •

But she's already gone. In the spare room, Bec's stripping the bed.

Everything of Mia's has disappeared except the cell phone still plugged into the wall. I pull it from the socket and switch it on. It beeps three times as I walk to Mum's car. I read the new messages.

Mia, come home. We can sort it out. I'm still your mother.

Don't hate me. It's not my fault.

I love you Mia.

I look for her at the bus stop but the seats are empty. There's another two hours before the bus will come.

I drive each street in town. The blond wig is easy to spot. For a girl who's running away, she's picked a strange place to stand. I pull the car over and watch.

Holding on to crutches, she's reading the posters in the window of the police station. It's like she's looking for someone. That's when it hits me that despite everything she says, Mia might actually want to be found.

I cross the road and step up to join her. By her side, I read the posters too, wondering if these people want to stay missing, or if they're just too proud or scared to turn back.

"Cam died."

"I knew him," she says after a while. "He asked me to play pool."

"Did you?"

"No. I should've, though. He was . . . sweet. I'm sorry."

We're speaking to each other's reflections in the glass. We could be ghosts.

I tell her I'm going to the service.

"Why?"

"He was a friend. It's in Perth. There's room for you."

She closes her eyes as her head drops. *Can't,* she mouths.

Mia's too far gone for choices. I have to make this one for her.

I ease the crutches free and place them against the window, then hook an arm under her knees and hoist her up. She lets me carry her to the car. She's heavier than I expected. Her skin is warm and kind of clammy. I hadn't noticed how sick she is.

I jog back for the crutches and that's when I see the photo on the left side of the window. The girl smiles out, with glossed lips, perfect teeth, and dark, shiny hair.

**Missing: MIA PHILLIPS, 17yo, female.
Amputee, needs treatment. Last seen at friend's
house in Perth.**

I drive home to grab a change of clothes. Mia stays in the
front seat. When I come back out, my mum's beside the driver's
door. I promise her we'll be safe. I'll watch out for roos. I'll drive
carefully with regular stops and stay overnight at Aunt Trish's
house. Mum hugs me through the window, then hands me my
pill box. What else can she do?

"I hope you feel better," she tells Mia, passing across a bag
of pears. "These are for your mum. And you. They're good."
Mum wants to say more, but she stops herself and kisses me
instead. I'm proud of her.

"See you soon."

• • •

I've made this trip north hundreds of times, but always with
Mum filling the hours with dialogue. This time I drive with
Mia beside me. She dozes most of the time. When she's awake,
the silence is comfortable, like an old blanket between us.

At a gas station I fill up the car and buy us bacon and egg
sandwiches and iced coffees. She sips hers through a straw,
looking over the countryside, which is dotted with cows.

Each time we close in on a town, Mia scans for radio
signals. We listen to whatever's playing until the reception
crackles again and she turns it off.

I think about Cam. Last year when our chemo cycles overlapped, he tried to "educate" my music tastes during our pool-playing marathons. He told me stories about girls and surfing. He'd always start with "When I was your age . . ." He was only thirty-two. He knew a lot about Buddhism. He said it helped put things into perspective. He would line up his cue and let it rest off the white ball for ages. He had composure when it mattered, even with that tumor branching out, taking hold.

"It shouldn't be quiet," I say aloud, unexpectedly.

Mia reaches for the radio dial, mistaking me.

"Cancer, I mean." The "c" word. With the destruction it brings, cancer should come howling into a body with sirens wailing and lights flashing. It shouldn't be allowed to slink in and take root in someone's brain like that, hiding among memories.

"Yeah."

Even though Mia doesn't say much, I'm glad she's here. Our decisions are easy ones. *Bathroom stop at this rest area or the next? Doritos or chili Grain Waves? Coke or iced coffee?*

Mia chooses iced coffee again. As I line up to pay, I see her frowning at the contents of a hot food case.

"You hungry?" I ask.

"Is that food?"

"Maybe forty percent of it. The rest . . . not sure. You've never had a corn dog?"

She shakes her head. "A corn dog? No. Have you?"

"Not one that looks so . . . last Tuesday."

"Chicken."

"I can't tell."

"I mean *you*," she says, like it's a dare.

So I buy us two corn dogs, even though they'd definitely be on my banned foods list. The guy packets them and checks out Mia's crutches.

"What happened?"

"Shark," she says, squeezing ketchup over her corn dog before I can stop her.

"Wow."

She winks. "If I were you, I'd think twice before peeing in your wetsuit."

The look on the guy's face as Mia swings away: priceless.

I don't know what tomorrow will bring. I don't know if she'll go home, or back to the hospital, or even back to the bus station to start her escape all over again.

But today, we eat salty, soggy corn dogs in the sunshine and they taste better than anything. Mia's got a knack for keeping me in the surprising, glaring present. Exactly where I'm supposed to be.

28
Mia

I hate Perth. I hate its suburbs, where every landmark pricks me with reminders.

I hate arriving, the engine turning off. The itch of my scalp beneath the sweaty wig. I hate the thought of getting out of the car, with its chip packets and the seat that's softened to my shape.

"You still okay with this?"

I shrug. What else can I do?

"We can find a motel, if you want. I've got enough cash."

"Your aunt's place will be fine," I say. Right now, I'm preoccupied by the clock on the dashboard. I calculate there's an hour and a half before I can take the next pills. Until then, I shouldn't be making snap decisions.

We're parked on a street that runs from King's Park down to the Swan River. On either side are high-rise apartment buildings, competing for views. I've never known anyone who lives near here.

"You didn't mention your aunt's a yuppie."

"She's not so bad . . ."

I give him a throwaway smile to show that I'm joking. It's only a gesture, but there's something about Zac's face that hooks my glance and keeps it there. For some reason, he seems older. Better. I blink in surprise.

It makes him self-conscious. "What?"

Perhaps his face is like the night sky, the way it changes each time you look away.

"What!?" Zac flips down the mirror and checks between his teeth.

"You look . . . different."

"Tired different? Just-driven-over-five-hundred-kilometers different? Or a-booger-in-my-nose different?"

Nope, he's the same Zac.

He swipes at his nose and I snort out a laugh. I don't know how he does it—how he makes me forget the clock and the pain. Sometimes, even if it's just for a few seconds, I can forget how crap my life is.

"Come on, booger-head. I gotta pee."

"Again? Are you taking the piss?"

"It's the iced coffees."

He offers me an empty Coke bottle.

"I had a catheter in after the surgery," I tell him. "I could pee into a bag anytime I wanted without leaving the bed."

"Nice."

"You know, I was actually kind of sad when they took it out. Going to a toilet is a total waste of time."

"Well, if you didn't drink so many iced coffees—"

"Thanks for those. I owe you."

"I know, I'm keeping a tab. The corn dog, though, that was on me."

● ● ●

We walk past the main gate and through a lush garden. In the center is a circular fountain with a concrete fish spitting out water. We avoid the splash and head to the entrance, where Zac buzzes the intercom. The response comes from a balcony six stories up.

"Zacky!" A woman waves, leaning dangerously over. "The lift's getting fixed so walk on up."

Zac turns to me. "You still good?"

"Maybe," I say, looking up.

He takes my backpack and leads the way through the foyer and into the stairwell.

"Take your time," he says. Like I have a choice.

With each step, the crutches dig harder into my armpits. Even the slightest weight on my left leg shoots fire up it. There's no forgetting myself anymore.

After the first ten steps, I pause on the landing. My arms are shaking when I pull strands of wig from my lips.

"Mia." My name echoes in the stairwell as Zac jumps down three steps.

I don't want him to see me like this, sweaty and stressed. I don't want him to see how much this hurts. Each step is a blinding flash.

"I'm fine."

But by the third floor, he's got his hand on my back. By the fourth, I'm leaning on him.

"I'll carry you," he offers at the fifth.

"You're not tough enough," I taunt, closing my eyes to the burn. Beneath my jeans, the stump throbs twice its size. The pain could set me alight.

At the sixth floor, the woman waits by an open door.

"Jeepers," she says, noticing my crutches. "You've done well. Is it your ankle?"

"Volleyball injury."

"Nasty."

Trish is toned and tanned. Barefoot, she wears a charcoal skirt and a cream blouse, with a thin gold necklace. She smells of flowers, just a bit, the kind of flowers you have to lean in to. She hugs Zac, then shakes my hand.

"It's good to meet you. Zac's told me a lot—"

"Not much—"

"A little about you. You've been staying at the farm?"

"Mia's an old friend," he says.

My breath is steadying but the nausea remains. This stupid leg shouldn't hurt so much, should it?

"I'm sorry about Cam. It's not fair—"

Zac drums his stomach. "I'm starving. Mia?"

I nod, though the idea of food makes me want to puke. "Starving."

"Zac knows I'm no domestic goddess, so I've prepared these." Trish presents three takeaway menus like prizes. "Mexican, Vietnamese, Italian."

"Mia?" Zac's beside me. Sweat trickles down the side of my face and I think he sees it. He helps me to a couch. I let him.

"Geez, do you need anything?"

I wave Trish away. "Mexican?"

"It's a ten-minute walk."

"I'll wait here. You two go. Do they do tortillas?"

"The best."

Zac crouches close, though I can't meet his gaze.

"What do you need?"

"Avocado. Extra cheese."

"What *else* do you need?"

I inhale. Fight the tears that want to come.

"Does your aunt have a bath?"

Zac shakes his head. "It's a small apartment."

"Then a glass of water and my backpack."

• • •

The apartment is beautiful, but it's the long wall of glass panes that's most appealing. I limp across and slide open the door. Cool wisps of breeze find my face. From the balcony, I watch Zac and Trish make their way down the street.

I've lived in Perth all my life but I've never seen it from this angle. Beside the river, cyclists ride in twos and threes. Lone joggers pound the pavement. Birds unfold their wings like flashers. Boats skip along the flat, wide water, racing the light home.

Along the freeway, red taillights nudge south. Inbound, white headlights stream over the bridge, heading north. From here, I can track the layout of suburbs. I can even guess where mine would be. My mum's. It's southwest of here, far from the river, past the freeway and farther inland, past the university and across Manning Highway, four streets down, then two to the right. A small, shadeless cul-de-sac with overgrown and squat orange villas for foreign students and single mothers.

If I had a telescope, I could probably find the house from here. I'd see its courtyard with plastic furniture. Its clothesline with three rows of pegged uniforms.

And if I looked inside, I might even see my mother there, with the pantry door open, finding nothing worth eating. Would the washing machine be thumping? Would the house seem even smaller with only one person in it?

People and birds turn to silhouettes. The sky is changing, throbbing with dusk. I know these colors well. Puckered pinks and flaming reds, hot and soft to touch. Scarlet smearing the horizon. A symphony of infection and pain. Then slowly, heavily, a violet descends like a giant bruise until it's all the same. There's a peace that comes with the dark. I exhale with relief. Without the rage of day, there's nothing left to feel.

The freeway unblocks itself. Lights twinkle. Cars stream to where they belong.

Six stories below, garden lights flicker on. I lean over the balcony, pushing my chest into the aluminum railing the way Trish did. The great gray fish continues to spit from its pond. I watch the water arc up and out, bubbling and then tumbling into its circular base. The water looks cold, and I imagine the relief it would give me. It would put out the fire. It would probably do more than that.

If I fell from here, six stories would be enough, wouldn't it? If I toppled into that cool concrete pond, I wouldn't burn anymore. I wouldn't be ugly. I wouldn't be so horrible and hopeless.

But it would be Zac and Trish who would find me, and I couldn't do that to them. I don't want Zac to be broken as well.

I don't know how this will end. The cancer didn't kill me, but it should've. Perhaps it'll come back, somewhere else, the way Cam's did. Perhaps the infection in my leg will finish me off, leaching enough poison into my bloodstream to end it. Or maybe a bus will take me so far, I can fall off the edge and Zac won't be around to pick up my pieces.

I see him walking up the hill with his aunt, lit by the street-lights. He carries a bag with tortillas, with extra avocado and cheese.

Poor Zac. He still thinks he can save me.

• • •

Lying on my side on the couch, I watch occasional headlights trace the curves of the river.

Trish had offered me the spare bed, but I insisted on the couch. It's the cool breeze I craved, so I kept the glass door open. Now I lie in T-shirt and undies, awake at one a.m. The last pain-killers have worn off completely.

I don't want to use up my supply, so I feel my way to the bathroom, where I close the door behind me and switch on the light. The cabinet is beneath the sink. I lower myself to the floor.

The cupboard is stacked: six packets of painkillers, five co-deine, anti-inflammatories, and heaps of sleeping tablets. I can't believe it. There's enough in here to numb a battlefield. There'd be enough to finish it all.

"There's more if you need."

I launch myself across my leg, but it's too late to cover it.

"Shut the door," I spit, swiveling. The light's too harsh for this. I need my jeans. My wig. "What are you doing?"

Trish's response is unexpected. "Sorry, Mia. I'm out of antibiotics."

I drag a towel from the rail to hide myself.

"No. I need codeine."

Trish lifts a packet from the floor, opens it, and pops two pills through the casing.

"Take them. Then tomorrow, see a doctor—"

"Doctors are assholes," I say. "You're not a doctor, are you?"

She shakes her head. "Lawyer. Though a lot of them are assholes too."

Leaning across me, Trish fills a glass with tap water, then crouches and hands it to me. I wash the pills down.

"It won't always hurt so much," she says. "It gets better."

What the fuck? She can't be serious. The last thing I need now is a lecture.

"You learn to live . . ."

I glare at the tiles, incredulous. What would this woman know, with her pedicured feet and toned calves? Who is she to counsel me on *learning to live*? How dare she keep looking at me, without the decency to turn away.

She must be in on it too. Zac's mum must've phoned her: *Keep an eye on the girl, she'll raid your cabinet like she did Bec's. Tell her to get her checkups and go back to her mother. Keep her away from my boy.*

I can't speak for outrage. For shame.

Trish eases herself to the tiles beside me, leaning her back against the shower cubicle. She stretches her legs out to the wall. Then she peels another two pills from the packet, places them on her own tongue, and swallows dry.

The fluorescent light doesn't flatter Trish either, I notice. She looks sunken—almost concave. Her camisole seems to hang on her, flattened against her chest the way it shouldn't. Where her thin gold necklace had sat before, just above her breasts, there's . . . nothing.

"Have you heard the story about the family who moved from Melbourne to Darwin, and then six years later the cat showed up, like nothing had happened?"

I shake my head. In this light, her skin is pale and uneven. Blotched in the inner arms. Puckered at the neck. Like Zac's. Like mine.

"Even after six years, I still think there's a cat heading to my door."

The codeine trickles into my bloodstream, bringing the promise of relief.

"I still get headaches. Insomnia. I still worry. But I don't . . . *hurt* like that anymore. I don't hurt . . . like you."

My words come out as a confession. "I hurt all the time."

"There are some things you can't change," Trish says, inspecting her arms. "And there are some things you can."

The drugs flood me, swamping my leg and its pain. But my chest, fuck, it still burns.

"It's not fair, hon." Trish speaks in Zac's voice. In mine. "It's not fair."

"It's not . . ."

"No, hon, it's *not* fair."

"It's *not* . . ."

"It's not fair . . ."

Our voices overlap and I let the tears fall as I'm rocked like a baby in the ugly light.

• • •

In the morning I clip on the leg, pull on jeans, brush out the wig. I steal some more painkillers only to find two fresh boxes already in my backpack.

Trish brings lattes and pancakes to the balcony, but I can't meet the eye of this woman, made womanly again with a wool knit top. At the table, Trish and Zac pass each other plates and maple syrup. They talk about school, the baby alpaca, and the new Italian coffee grinder, as if these things matter. I watch them, two relatives with unlucky genes, discussing coffee beans.

How the hell do they do it? He's got someone else's marrow and she has a butchered chest. How do they coast through each day with this illusion of control? Ever since my surgery, all I've done is swing from pity to rage. Pity to rage. How can I not? Everywhere I look I'm reminded of what's missing.

My instinct is to howl at the joggers below. I imagine breaking their legs and clawing out their hair. Why should they be so lucky? So obliviously lucky? And those cyclists, riding in symmetry—I want to push them off their bikes. I want to punch anyone who dares to be happy.

I watch Trish playing with her necklace, and I wonder where she hides all her anger. I study her face and her hands, but I can't find it. Has she forgotten what it's like? Or has she become an expert at pretending?

She slides a pancake onto my plate. "Go on. It's the one thing I can actually cook."

What if all this—the crocheted tablecloth, the breakfast rituals and small talk—is just pretend? Is Zac in on it too, faking normal? If so, the world should stand up and clap and give them both Academy Awards.

I try to take their lead. I swallow the coffee. It's too strong, but I don't complain. I add more milk. I hold my tongue. I count to ten. To twenty. I mirror the way they spread butter and pour maple syrup. I take another pancake. I lean forward on my elbows and, like them, I let the sun find my face. I fake a smile and I think they buy it.

Before we leave, I put on lip-gloss and a brave face. I draw my crutches close, arming myself. Today I need to pretend, because today isn't about me. It's about Zac and his memory of Cam. I'm just along for the ride.

29
Zac

Fifty meters out, men and women sit on boards with their legs dangling. They're easy bait, but sharks must know better than to hunt this coast today.

Cam's service is taking place out there, but Mia and I are up in the dunes. She keeps getting bogged in the sand.

She chucks the crutches. "Useless."

"You need four-wheel-drive ones."

She flops onto the sand and I join her.

"No, Zac. Get down there before it's over."

"Says who?"

"We've come all this way."

To be honest, I don't really want to be in that crowd in the sea. They'd be friends of Cam's from way back, long before his tumor.

He was a mate, I can imagine them saying. *A character. A legend.* I'd feel like a fraud.

"Go on. He'd like it."

"Who?"

"Cam."

"Cam? He'll be halfway to Rottnest Island by now."

Mia's eyes bulge. "You can't say that."

"He can't hear us."

"Shhh. He can so."

"Cam!" I shout, startling a guy walking past. "Safe travels, mate. Send me a postcard from Indonesia."

Mia punches me.

"Hey, Cam, do you remember this chick from Room Two? Yeah, the drama queen who hits like a girl."

Mia pulls a towel over her head like a tepee.

I nudge her. "Cam says hello." But I can't see her expression.

The thing is, I've thrown enough corpses over fences to know that nothing happens when you die. There are no trumpets or rising up of spirits. Sheep don't go to heaven and goats don't go to hell. It's just flesh turned cold, soon to be another step in a food chain where nothing is wasted. There's nothing mysterious about death or what comes after. There's just nothing. Whatever's left of Cam is drifting northwest in the Leeuwin Current, being nibbled at and shat out by fish.

"After my grandma died, she came to visit me." Mia's voice comes from inside her towel. "I woke up in the night and she was there."

"Your grandma?"

"Her shape. But I knew it was her. It felt like she'd come to check on me. I said, 'Grandma?' And then she walked backwards, until she ... vaporized. I don't know what happens, Zac, but there's more than this. People stay around for a while.

Sometimes there's too much energy in a room. Cam's still here—"

"Then go play pool with him."

Mia stomps her right foot. "Cam is here and he reckons you're being a fuckwit."

I laugh. She's right about one thing, at least. I lean back onto my fists, looking out to the sea. I should be grateful for this: a beach, the use of the car, and Mia, who's just trying to be kind.

"I miss him," I admit to the ocean. "I wish I'd gone for that surf."

Two girls in bikinis make a detour around us, whispering. Mia's head tracks them, and then she lies on her back, the towel still in place.

"Mia?"

"Don't use my name."

"You know them?"

"They know me. They're from school."

The girls stop farther down the beach and sit down. Mia peers at them through a gap in her towel. "Cellulite."

"I didn't notice."

"Do you think they're cute?"

"Nothing special."

"Do you like them?"

"No."

The towel falls away. Below the blond bangs, Mia's brown eyes stare up at me.

"Why do you like me?"

With the palm of my hand, I smooth crescents into the sand.

Why do I like Mia?

I like that she's tough on me, knowing I can handle it. She doesn't tiptoe around the bad stuff or hide what's going on in her head. If she feels something, she says so. She *shows* it. She says and does all the things others hold back. She's not predictable or safe. She doesn't talk bullshit, the way most other girls do. She's alive, despite everything, kicking and screaming and swearing. Fighting, still.

"Zac?"

"Because you don't have cellulite," I say.

She blinks. "What about my shit-hot sense of humor?"

Yeah, there's that, too, those razor-edged comments that come from nowhere like nunchuks. She's smarter than she gives herself credit for.

She squints at me for a while. "I like you, Zac, because you treat me like I'm up here." Her hand makes a circular motion around her face, like she's a model on *The Price Is Right*. "And not down there."

"You're not your leg, Mia."

"And the other reason I like you is that you're good to your friends. So shut the hell up, stand the fuck up, walk down that beach, and say goodbye to Cam from both of us."

I do as she says, even though the service is falling apart now. People are pointing their boards to the shore, some lying, some standing, until they're scooped up in the shallow palms of waves, gliding to the sand, where they step off and shake out with a laugh.

Nina's on the shore. She meets me halfway, shoes in hand.

"You made it, Zac."

"Yeah."

"It's good you came. You look great." Mascara's made smudges under her eyes.

"Helga delivered after all."

"Patrick says you got a Make-A-Wish. What are you asking for?"

"I'm still hoping Emma Watson's free . . ."

"Fingers crossed. You've done well, Zac. Cam would be proud."

It's "proud" that does it. For some reason, the word plugs my throat. I try to swallow but I can't. My eyes sting.

"He always liked you, Zac."

C for Cam didn't deserve to die and I don't know if he's watching or not as I let the tears come and let Nina hug me. I imagine him dying quick and hard, still gripping the steering wheel, his chest ripping apart. Did he realize those were his final, liberating breaths? Did he regret anything in those seconds, or did he smile and welcome it and go fearlessly to wherever he is now?

God, of course I want Mia to be right. I want to believe that Cam goes on, that he's here in this hug, or better yet, out riding the next wave. Anywhere but nowhere.

Nina holds me tight. In the distance, I see Mia. Standing with her crutches, she's looking at the dunes with fear.

• • •

I wait out in front of the shops holding two kebabs, a Coke, and an iced coffee. Mia's been ages in the public restrooms. I hope she hasn't done a runner.

But she finally emerges with Nina.

Once she's made it up the path, I ask her if she wants to see a movie. I'm not ready to drive her home, or to a bus station, or anywhere else that's final. She says she can't.

When I offer her the kebab and iced coffee, she shakes her head and looks at the concrete. She's already somewhere else.

"I'm tired, Zac."

"Actually, there's this place I know . . ."

But she turns and retraces the path to where Nina is waiting. Her crutches remind me of the first *tap, tap, tap*ping of her knuckles on the hospital wall.

A lonely Morse code.

And there's not a thing I can say in reply.

PART THREE
Mia

30
Mia

Where ru Mia?

With Nina

Where ru going? I'll come.

Go home Zac.

In Emergency, a doctor takes my temperature and looks at
my leg. He writes in a folder, then phones for a wheelchair. Nina
pushes me along the ground floor to an elevator, where there's
a map of the hospital, with eight levels and color-coded areas.
Oncology is lime green, but we don't go there. She wheels me
inside and presses the button for level three. We go to the blue
ward, for infections and burst appendices.

"You're not a cancer patient anymore," Nina reminds me.

My cancer's gone. The ultrasounds and blood tests prove it,
though I have to check them over to be sure.

They hook me to a drip, then phone my mum—I'm only seventeen, after all. She's here in twenty minutes and stays, sleeping in the reclining chair at night. She doesn't ask where I've been, if I'll run away again, or if I'll follow the doctors' orders. She buys us magazines. Sometimes she stands by the window, looking out over the street.

"You can go have a smoke," I tell her. But she says she's trying to give it up.

Zac calls but I don't feel like answering. I don't want him to hear how sad I am. After all my talk of adventure, I'm back in the hospital, like a fool.

A prosthetist fits me for a permanent socket and gives me another "How to Care for Your New Prosthetic" booklet. I'd thrown the first one away. She tells me the new leg, when it's made, will be better than the temp. I'm supposed to wear it for only an hour each day for the first week, building up week by week, to break it in.

She inspects the wound. "You should've had this looked at. The temp was a bad fit."

Understatement of the year.

A PT teaches me to bandage myself. He shows me how to roll on the silicon lining. He's young and cute, and careful when he touches me.

"It's okay," I tell him. "It's better than it was."

After a week, I'm prescribed antibiotics, anti-inflammatories, and antidepressants. Mum pays the pharmacist and drives us home.

Mum's knowledge of the last few months is sketchy. She knows that I was given weekend leave and spent one night at home, then took off with a fistful of drugs, money, and a change of clothes. I stayed with girlfriends, who made tea and toast, then came home plastered after clubbing to tell me their dirty, guilty secrets. Hungover, they phoned my mum to say I was safe. She would've guessed I went to Rhys's house next. I slept on his couch because my leg hurt too much to share his bed. Rhys was the only one who knew the truth, but he withdrew. Became distant. He didn't have the guts to deal with this. He wasn't the man I thought he was.

When I enter my bedroom, it looks like someone else's. Silver high heels are on the table, where they've been for thirteen weeks. My formal dress glitters from a curtain rod, its beads glinting, waiting for the old Mia to step in and zip it up, to pose in front of the mirror, judging the best angles. Had I really loved this dress? It seems too loud now. It's still got the price tag hanging from it.

Mum cooks honey chicken drumsticks. My childhood favorite. We eat in front of the TV, watching whatever's on.

It's hard to be home, but running takes effort. I don't have the energy. I can't even think about tomorrow. All I want to do is sleep.

My bed doesn't feel right, though. The last time I slept here I had two feet at the end of me. I'm like Goldilocks in the three bears' house. Everything is too big, too small, too hard, too soft.

I turn off the lamp. The room switches to black, but soon a soft light glows by my bed. I watch as the star takes shape on my wall. I must have stuck it here, that night I left the hospital.

Zac. He's one thing, at least, I can count on.

· · ·

I get good at passing time.

Eleven hours are for sleeping (including an afternoon nap), three for watching TV, two for eating (one spent getting up and checking the fridge and closing it again), two hours online, one for reading magazines, and two for the DVD Mum brings home each day.

And the other three hours? I'm not sure. Daydreaming, maybe. Imagining the imprint my body makes on carpet.

The sound of the postman is the only thing to lure me out of the house. Each afternoon, I put on the wig, grab my crutches, and make my way to the mailbox, which is usually empty. I sometimes see people sitting at the bus stop nearby. I notice how easily they walk up the bus's four steps. You never think of your legs when there are two of them. I don't hate these people anymore. I don't want to break their legs. These days, it's not rage I feel, or pity. There's just . . . nothing.

Weeks pass, I think. I don't count them.

I sit on my floor with the wardrobe doors open. Shelves are jammed with clothes and shoes and heaps of crap I'd forgotten: jigsaw puzzles, fancy-dress costumes, letters from old boyfriends, collector cards, crumbly makeup, and other strange gifts from friends. I throw most of the stuff in the wheelie bin. I tidy the wardrobe and take stock of what's left. I cry. Then I pull it all out of the bin.

One day, I notice a child's wading pool in the neighbors' pile of rubbish. It's still there at night, so I ask Mum if she'll drag it back for me. I clean it the next morning in our courtyard, then fill it with water. It's not as long or deep as Bec's bathtub, but I can lie in it, limbs draped over the edges, watching the clouds drift across the sky. Sometimes I read a book. Other times I doze. There's nothing I have to do.

Some days I sit on Mum's bed, seeing myself in her mirror. I try on her earrings and spray her perfume. I have enough hair for her clips to hold on to. There are more clothes in her wardrobe than in mine. The left side is for her work clothes. The right, going out. The black dresses aren't as black as they used to be. There are peg marks on her tops. Why doesn't she chuck the old clothes away?

I pull two photo albums from a shelf and lie on her bed with them. I'm intrigued by younger versions of myself: a fat baby in disposable diapers, a pink ribbon in my hair. Occasionally there are glimpses of Mum. She was only sixteen, younger than I am. Her eyes shy from the camera. When she's holding me, her expression seems to be asking, *Where did you come from?*

There are ancient photos of vacations, mostly with Grandma and Grandpa and their siblings. I am seven or eight beside a little boat they called a tinny. I remember a Queensland uncle showing me how to snatch the empty milk carton from the river and then pull at the rope, hand after hand, until a crab pot came, dripping, from the water. Often it only held the snarled bones wired inside as bait. But sometimes it had a vicious crab, as brown and murky as the mangroves. The great-uncle—who's long dead now—would whoop like crazy. He showed me how to grab the flailing back legs and squeeze them together, to lift the angry crab into the air and drop it in the lidded bucket. I would hear it clack and dance for hours.

Sometimes, as we pulled a crab from the pot, a leg or claw

would get left behind, gripping at netting. We'd toss the pot back in, tempting other animals with displaced body parts.

Then we'd feast at night. We'd smash open fat claws and suck sweet juice from skinny legs. Even without the absent limbs, there was always enough to go around. Perhaps that's why crabs have so many legs (eight) and claws (two). Some are bound to be torn away.

In a street next to mine, there's a man whose arm was ripped off by a meatpacking machine long ago. In primary school, we'd wonder about him—*How does he tie shoelaces? Eat his dinner?*—more with curiosity than horror. We'd try to glimpse him in his garden, watching his sleeve sway as he watered his lawn. I remember, too, the girl in kindergarten who was born with stubs for fingers. And on TV last year, after the Olympics wound down, there was a whole army of paralympians marching and wheeling across the screen. I didn't pay much attention at the time.

We're all just crabs, marching. So many missing pieces.

I switch off the TV and check the fridge. I check my cell phone again. Nothing.

Twenty-four hours are easy to pass now that I know how.

31
Mia

I take my first unaided step, but no one's here to see it. I take two more, then grab for the kitchen bench. Almost eighteen and learning to walk again. It's got to be harder than the first time.

Mum's at work, but it's Zac I want to share this with. *Look, no hands!* Zac would get what a big deal it is.

In the last week or so, there have been other things I've wanted to tell him. Mostly small stuff, like a song on a radio, or a cooking show that used dukkah in a recipe. This morning I made pancakes, thinking of him. I almost texted him a photo.

I didn't, though. I thought it might be weird, after two months of silence, to send a photo of a pancake.

Zac had phoned and texted every day for ages before giving up. I should've replied, but I didn't. I had nothing worth saying. *Empty. Still empty.* No one wants to hear that.

But today, I've taken three steps without crutches and I'm busting to tell him.

I sit down and draft a message. I draft at least ten of them, deleting them all. One hundred and sixty characters won't do what I want them to.

So I lock the front door behind me. I walk to the post office using my crutches—a kilometer without them would be way too ambitious. I wear the wig and a hat, in case someone recognizes me.

In the post office, I take my time inspecting the tacky postcard display. I choose one with a photo of a river and a black swan.

> Hey Zac
>
> How is the olive farm? How's the little alpaca? Or is it a big alpaca? How are the ferrets and the crazy chickens? And how's Bec? Did she have a boy or a girl?
>
> In a week I turn eighteen, like you. I'm still getting the hang of this walking business, so I'll play it safe and stay home. Clubbing could be dangerous.
>
> I signed back into Facebook the other day. Where were you, eh? Guess you were sleeping, like normal people . . . You haven't updated in a while. Are you over Facebook now, or too busy with year 12? Either way, sign back in, OK? Who else will I chat to at stupid hours?
>
> Good luck with your mock exams.
> Mia

I stick a stamp to it, but there are too many reasons not to drop it into the box. What if Zac's mum reads the postcard and doesn't pass it on? What if he doesn't miss me the way I miss him? What if he hates me for not responding earlier, or worse, what if he's forgotten me altogether and I sound like a dumb-ass?

I walk home, the postcard mocking me in my pocket.

I reach the entrance to the villas at the same time as the postman. Seated on his bike, he slides mail into each of the slots. I take the postcard from my pocket and, before I can stop myself, hand it to him. He pops it into his tray as if this is a usual exchange, then shoots off, his bike stop-starting away from me, the postcard going with it. *Shit*.

Perhaps courage is simply this: spur-of-the-moment acts when your head screams *don't* but your body does it anyway.

Courage, or stupidity. It's hard to tell.

. . .

The volunteer at the cancer center smiles like she remembers me, but she couldn't—I never came down here. It was Mum who collected a few wigs for me to borrow. They were all ugly but I chose the blond one because it resembled me the least. I wasn't supposed to keep it this long.

The wig's kind of grotty so the woman puts it limply in a bag.

"I hope Rhonda behaved herself."

"Rhonda?"

"She's a cutie, but trouble."

"They have names?"

On faceless styrofoam heads are wigs of all lengths, styles, and colors. I see that each has a label: Pam, Marguerite, Vikki, Patricia.

The woman touches my hair like it's public property. "Beautiful. You look like an actress."

"Which one?"

"Plenty."

Before cancer, my friends and I would complain about split ends, and the cost of products and haircuts every eight weeks. The damage from hair straighteners. Hair was something we took for granted.

Now, five months after chemo, my hair's grown back healthy. It seems a lighter color than before.

"Brazil nut brown," the hairdresser said yesterday, running her fingers through it. "Nice. Just a trim?"

I nodded. I'd forgotten what to say.

"A few centimeters off? Or are you wanting to grow it out?"

"I think I'm growing it out."

"Do you want some layering at the back? For body?"

I stammered. I may have snorted. "I don't care." I hadn't expected to be given choices.

"And a bit of layering around the face for shape?"

The hairdresser had no idea why I was laughing. Then crying. But she snipped my hair expertly as I rubbed at sudden tears. I wanted to watch it all. Brazil nut brown falling to the floor.

And today, I look like an actress, apparently. There are layers near my cheekbones, with a bit of a curl at my neck. My hair is back, despite everything that's happened. My eyebrows and eyelashes are like normal. My period continues to return, again and again, and I'm weirdly pleased when it does. Even chocolate now tastes the way it should.

An Indian girl, maybe ten years old, wheels through the door with a pink scarf knotted around her head. She's followed by her mother. On the girl's lap is a copy of *James and the Giant Peach*.

She's had cancer for a while; she knows the woman by name. Despite the shadows beneath her eyes, the girl's skin is luminous.

"Hello, Shani, how are you today?"

"Good."

"So then . . . who do you want to be this week?"

The girl unknots her scarf and I turn away, letting them carry out the dress-up game.

I swing past the pamphlets for wheelchair basketball, counselors, makeovers, art therapy sessions, Make-A-Wish awards, amputee groups, and bereavement services. I swing out to the bus stop, where two old men and a woman sit waiting.

So then . . . who do I want to be this week?

A woman rides past on a Vespa. She has a shiny blue helmet and a spotted scarf blowing behind her. She uses her hands to steer and brake—her feet, I notice, don't have to do a thing.

I want to be her, I think. I want to be moving again.

• • •

Four days later and still no reply. Maybe I got his address wrong on the postcard. Maybe he's too busy with exams. Maybe the postman didn't send it after all.

I check my cell, but there's nothing new. It's only on Facebook that I find an unread message.

But it's not from Zac.

Miiiia. Had a few mixers tonight but they weren't the same without you :-(How's Sydney? Are you finishing the beauty course?
I quit school, did you know? I'm working at a bank now, not far
from your mum's place. The uniform sucks but at least I get paid
;-) Bloody miss you. Shay xx

And it hits me that I miss her too.

• • •

Two days on and the mailbox remains empty. It upsets me, so I
keep on walking. Without crutches, I make my way around the
block. I'm back too soon so I do it again, farther past the post
office and the row of shops.

I stop outside the bank and peer in. Shay's standing behind
a teller's desk. She looks good in the uniform, with her hair
pulled back like that. She seems different from the crazy best
friend I had through high school.

She doesn't recognize me, even when she says, "Next,
please" and I'm right in front of her. The smile stays frozen on
her face for three complete seconds. "Fuck. Mia? For real?"

"Hi, Shay."

"What are you doing?"

"I'm here for a loan."

"For real? You're not in Sydney? Hang on, I'm nearly on
lunch. Come with?"

I can almost keep up with her on the dash to the café, where
we grab a table and a guy takes our order. It's harder to follow
the monologue about her job, but I try to make the right faces
when I'm supposed to.

"Your hair's great. Is that your natural color?"

I nod. "Brazil nut brown."

"Very specific. Thank god you got over that blond phase. It was too much, you know? In*tense*. Then you went away . . . Hey, I'm still with Brandon."

"Really?"

"I love him. Don't worry, Mia, I know you're not his . . . biggest fan."

"I didn't say that." Did I?

"I could tell."

I can't remember not liking Brandon, or at least, showing I didn't like him. He was harmless enough, when he wasn't butting in every five minutes.

"He used to try so hard to impress you."

"Me?" I snort. "Why?"

Shay's rubbing a sachet of sugar between her thumb and fingers. "Because you were my best friend, and you were hard to impress. You were *Mia Phillips*." She says my name as if it's special. "Everyone wanted to impress you. You know that."

I shake my head. I don't. I didn't. If Shay only knew the shit I've been dragged through since then. These days, I'm more impressed by simple things: waking up without pain, cute finds at thrift shops, and discovering that I still have a friend.

"I'm just Mia. I'm just . . . normal." At school I hated the word. Now it feels like a kind of a prize. Not a first prize, admittedly, but it's something.

"Normal? Normal, my ass, Mia. Why did you go to Sydney, anyway? There's got to be a guy involved."

I drink my vanilla milkshake. What lies beneath my jeans

and knee-high boots can remain a secret for now. So can Zac. God, I miss him. But I can't message him yet — it's his turn.

"So, about this loan."

"I'll chat to my people. What do you want it for?"

I grin. "A canary-yellow Vespa."

"Ha, told you! Normal. My. Ass."

32
Mia

There are seven hundred shades of matte paint in the hardware store. Eighty-two of them are blue. It's Blue Opulence that I keep coming back to. It's an early-morning blue. A blue that roosters crow to. A view-through-Zac's-window blue.

On my eighteenth birthday, I paint my room Blue Opulence. Mum offers to help and I show her how to cover the cornices and window frames with tape, the way Bec had. *A new coat of paint for a new soul,* Bec said when she painted the baby's room olive green.

"I want to paint the ceiling too."

Mum does it for me. She stands on my bed, which I've covered with newspaper. She's shorter than me, but steadier. Blue drops stain her hair and leave spots on her face. When she turns to me—to check that she's doing all right—I tell her she looks like a character from *Avatar*.

"From what?"

"We should get it on DVD tonight."

"It's your birthday," she says, as if I've forgotten.

I had. "Then get *two* bags of M&M's."

A homemade cake is on the kitchen table. Mum's spelled out *Happy Birthday Mia* with Smarties, the way she does every year.

When I turned eight, the cake mortified me. I saw the way my school friends—accustomed to princess cakes and butter-flies—exchanged critical glances. "What does it say?" asked one. The final two letters of my name were smaller than the rest, squeezed in as if my mother hadn't thought far enough ahead. On a plastic tablecloth were bowls of cheeses and salted nuts, but the girls wanted cookies and ice cream and pink soda. That day I realized how small the villa was. I noticed for the first time the marks on the carpet, the unhidden ashtrays, and the rust in the bathroom sink. I was embarrassed by the slimy soap in the hand basin, not like the bottles of hand soap other girls' mothers had, with fluffy hand towels. My mother was too young. She should have been going out with friends, drinking cocktails and flirting with men in bars, not surrounded by bois-terous eight-year-olds demanding musical chairs. Mum looked lost. That's when I knew I'd outgrown her.

This time last year, the cake was left untouched as I cel-ebrated my seventeenth in Fremantle with a dozen friends and a mix of ID cards, real and fake. We got hammered and I danced on a table until getting kicked out. I wore a black dress with a gold belt. I liked the looks I got from men outside cafés. I was good with heels. I liked the shouts from passing cars and the envy of midthirties women in jeans and cardigans leaving cine-mas. I liked the free vodkas I got from the bartender at the next club *Because it's my birthday!* and the way Rhys paid the cab-driver to drop us off at the park, where we ran, laughing, and made out near the kids' swing set. My ankle was sore then—I'd thought it was from dancing in my new heels. I ignored it for another four months. It was just an annoying ankle in a near-perfect world.

Shay phones, but she can't coax me out. I don't want to risk bumping into old friends after six months of avoiding them. I can't be bothered with makeup, or deciding what to wear.

All I want is to veg out in front of *Avatar*, but even that's not easy. Mum gets restless during the film, and it's not because she's eaten half the cake and most of the M&M's. I'd forgotten the main character has legs that don't work. On Earth he's a paraplegic, but on Pandora he can run in huge, loping strides. He falls in love with a sexy blue alien and never wants to leave.

Mum's anxious because I finished the antidepressants two weeks ago and haven't gone for a refill. Her eyes flicker my way, worried the film will be a trigger that sends me fleeing, admittedly in a hobbling, swaying kind of way. But it isn't.

A few months of being still have taught me I'm not in a Hollywood film. This Earth is the only one I have and I'm stuck on it, with my imperfect mother and a fiberglass leg. I know I'll always feel off-kilter, that I'll continually have to right myself. I know this now. Running away wouldn't change it. The east coast of Australia doesn't tilt to a different angle.

Later, I log in to Facebook. I speed-read my profile page, surprised by the number of birthday messages. But none is from Zac.

I can make excuses for the lack of a card, but there's no way of explaining this. He'd know it's my birthday—on Facebook, *everyone* knows. The only reason he'd miss it is the obvious one: he's forgotten me.

Maybe it only takes three months for *that*—generous arms, laughter under sheets, his bashful affection—to fade to this. Perhaps time eats away all relationships.

Perhaps in a few more months we'll be strangers.

I switch off my light. Zac wants to get on with his life. He wants me to leave him alone.

But that damn star keeps glowing, regardless.

33
Mia

I find a blaze of red roses on the doorstep, but the card has Mum's name on it. She puts a hand to her cheek when she reads it.

"Who is he?"

"Just a guy . . ."

"From the Internet?"

She shrugs, turning away.

"What's he like?"

"He's okay. Nothing special."

Before I got sick, Mum would go on dates with whoever asked. She kept men secret from me, or thought she did. To them she was an enigmatic potential girlfriend, but in private she was an anxious single mother who couldn't control her daughter. It's from her that I learned how to pretend, and how to switch faces for different audiences.

Sharing a small house was never easy. If I came home happy, she'd bring me down, out of jealousy, or spite. And vice versa. There was a constant seesawing of emotion, one of us always on edge. I knew she resented me for fucking up her life, and I hated her for being a fuckup. In public she'd embarrass me, so I learned to keep my distance. At home she was always in my face. I could never do anything right.

In the kitchen, Mum inhales the scent of roses. How come it's so easy for a man to make my mother smile? Why has it always been impossible for me?

A man exists who sees something good in my mother: a thirty-four-year-old woman who's just doing her best. A man likes her enough to buy a dozen red roses, handwrite her a note, and personally deliver them to our doorstep. That takes courage.

I fill a jug with water and arrange the roses. I want her to be happy, even though I'm lonely. I want my mum to be loved, even though I'm not.

Then she hugs me and I think, perhaps, I am.

• • •

When I go to check the mail four days later, a semi-trailer is blocking my path.

A man sets a ramp in place, jogs up into the truck, then wheels down a trolley that's holding a tree. Tied to the tree is a shovel. What the hell?

"Where do you want it?"

"Not there. Who's it for?"

He checks his clipboard. "Mia Phillips. That you?"

I nod. The tree's taller than me, with thick, swishy branches and silver-green leaves.

He shows me my name on his delivery schedule as proof.

"What do I do with it?"

"Beats me—I'm just the messenger."

When I sign the form I notice the truck's loaded with cardboard boxes stamped with THE GOOD OLIVE!.

"Are they full of oil?"

"Just the messenger." He offers to wheel the tree inside the villa and I let him. Then he does a noisy fifty-one-point turn to get out of our cul-de-sac.

"Mia?" Mum has to contort herself through the front door. "What's this?"

"It looks like a leccino. Or it could be a manzanillo. Hard to tell at this stage."

"A what?"

"An olive tree. We have to plant it."

"Why?"

"Because that's what you do with trees."

She takes off her shoes and inspects the trail of dirt on the carpet. "But why would anyone give us a *tree?*"

I smile. She still doesn't know about Zac, how it was either him or oblivion.

She finds a card in the pot and hands it to me. The front has a picture of a bright orange flower. Inside, the handwriting is unfamiliar.

Happy belated birthday, Mia. Hope you enjoyed yourself. We had to shift some fences and dig up a few trees. Thought you might find a home for this baby? Hope you're well. Wendy and all. x

I would've preferred a card from Zac, but it's something at least. I look again at the tree from his mum. Its soft leaves are offered in a truce.

"How do you look after an olive tree? Mia?"

"Don't stress, they're tough." I remember Zac's lecture from under the quilt. "Even if you neglect them for thousands of years, they'll still grow fruit—"

"Olives are fruit?"

I laugh. "We can Google it if you want. It just needs soil, water, and sun. Maybe some fertilizer."

"You know this?"

I shrug. "Little apple, little egg."

• • •

Between us, we drag the potted tree through the villa and outside. Mum has a date with the roses man and I tell her to go. I'm left in the courtyard with the strangest present I've ever received. It's enough to make me grab for my phone and type in a text.

> Hey Zac, say thanks to yr mum for me. Did u tell her it was my birthday? Very sweet, both of u. Any planting tips?? :-) Mia

There's so much else I'm desperate to say: That my walls and ceiling are blue. That my hair's touching my shoulders. That I think about him all the bloody time.

But I play it safe and just press "Send."

I keep the phone in my hand, expecting it to flash and vibrate at any moment. Minutes pass. I check it again and again, but the stupid thing stays mute. For so long.

Zac was once the knock to my tap, but now he's the boy who leaves me agonizing over a text message. He used to take my mind off the pain; now he's the one causing it. The silence is agony. It turns me into knots, making me doubt myself and everything he said. An hour and no reply. I'm sick with not knowing.

I shouldn't, I know, but I write another message. I don't censor anything.

> Zac, Im sorry I ignored u. I bottomed out. I was sad. Im getting better, but each time u ignore me, it bottoms me out again. Do u hate me? Have I lost u? I didnt mean to lose u. Dont be lost. Im sorry. Dont hate me.

I press "Send" and it's gone. Courage and stupidity, combined.

And still nothing comes back. One hour. Two. Three. The phone is a brick in my pocket. Without the buffer of antidepressants, there's nothing to stop me from sliding down that slope of self-hate again. I feel the pull of *ugly* and *unlovable* and *you stupid fucking girl, how could you believe he'd want you?* I feel them together—pity and rage. And I keep sliding down.

Fuck, I need to *do* something. I start to dig a hole. I follow the advice on the tree's tag and keep digging, even though the sun's gone down.

I get to fifty centimeters and dig farther. It cramps my knees and hips, but I go deeper, scooping out rocks. I have to *Keep busy*, like the cancer handbook says. I pull the tree closer and tip it over, levering it from its pot; then I get on my knees and force it in and upright, filling the space with loose, sinewy soil. I shove it in and push it down, using my forearms to move it around.

My body hurts when I finally stand. My skin's coated with dirt. I've lost track of hours: it's so late it could be tomorrow. I ache all over but I'm glad. I planted this. I've done something real.

The tree's my height now. Deep down, its roots will be probing, reaching for things to grip on to. But here at eye level, its branches are poised and still. Breathe, Mia, I tell myself. Be still.

When I shower, brown water swirls at my foot. It takes all my resolve not to hate myself. I decide to delete Zac's number from my phone. I have to. I don't have the strength for another rejection.

And tomorrow, I'll catch up with Shay. I might even email Tamara, my friend from primary school. When she went to a girls' school we drifted apart, though it was probably my fault. I'd like to see her. We can talk about year twelve, and boys, and whatever else matters to her. Anything to get out of the house and away from the disappointment of Zac.

Exhausted, I switch off the light and crawl cleanly into bed. I peel the glow-in-the-dark star from the wall and let it fall to the floor.

That's when my phone beeps beside me. Three a.m.

> I dont hate u Mia. Dont be sad. Im sorry, been busy.
> I have news.

34
Mia

The train slows and I tread to the middle, holding handrails as I pass them. A kid notices my slight limp and looks up in query.

"Leg went to sleep," I say, and he turns back to the window.

At Showgrounds Station, the doors open to the low mash of rock songs, loudspeakers, and generators. Even from here, I see metal cages pivot and plummet and tiny limbs flailing in waves. Beside me, kids squeal and jump onto the train platform, followed by parents with strollers.

I walk down the ramp behind them, closing in on the tunnel and the entrance to the grounds. Caterpillar lines wriggle toward the turnstiles. I step into line, the only one here alone, the only one more nervous than excited. What if I bump into someone from school?

The line shuffles along and there's only one reason I shuffle along with it.

It's in my back pocket.

Hi Mia

Howdy from Los Angeles, the home of Baywatch, fake tan, and guys on rollerblades. Dad and Evan are freaking out.

FYI, year 12's more hectic the second time. Plus pruning needed doing, Anton came back, and Bec had baby Stu. Somehow, I had to lock in my Make-A-Wish thing, so the day after exams I was on a plane for the US — LA, San Francisco, New York, then Disneyland. The whole fam's come along for the ride.

Yesterday we did a bus tour of famous people's fences. The driver spotted someone called Jane Fonda walking a dog. Evan swears he saw Arnie Schwarzenegger.

My phone doesn't have roaming but I'll send another postcard soon.

Hope you're good,

Zac

PS. Can you do us a favor? The Websters entered Sheba in the Perth Show and Bec wants a pic. Judging is the first Sunday, 2pm. I'll pay you back the entry fee . . . or I'll take it off your iced coffee bill ;-)

PPS. Our neighbor Miriam's going for a bake-off record — her fruit cake's won 10 years straight (using our citrus olive oil, of course).

PPPS. Have I mentioned Freddo show bags are my fave . . . ?

I've read this postcard a hundred times. It's brilliant to hear from him, even if he is on the opposite side of the world. More than anything, I'm stoked he hasn't forgotten me.

I hand over the twenty-dollar entry fee, then push through the turnstiles into air that's ripe with cinnamon sugar and sausage on a stick. Dirt clouds hover, kicked up by thousands of shoes. There's a stink of hay, too, of animals and shit. I don't recall the show being so rank, but then again, I've never walked in on my own.

Two years ago, there were twenty of us who arrived late on a Wednesday. Most of our time was spent in line for rides, followed by perfect minutes spent flying through air at all angles, trying desperately not to hurl or pee. We wandered through dusty alleyways, occasionally trying our luck with sideshow games. Before closing there was a frenzied rush of show bag purchases—SpongeBob SquarePants, Angry Birds, Freddo Frogs—and glow-in-the-dark gadgets. Waiting for the train, we inflated toys and decorated ourselves with plastic accessories, reminiscing about the years when show bags had quality items, and more of them.

In primary school, I came with Tamara and her big sister. We dared each other onto the roller coaster, then relived it laughingly for hours, choking on hot chips. Tamara's sister won her a big green dog in a game and I was impressed. I thought no one ever got to choose from the top row. I wanted it, of course—that green dog, a big sister. She could only win a small penguin for me, which I slept with until it burst.

When I was younger than that, the Ferris wheel was my favorite. I would slide into the space between Grandma and

Grandpa. I loved the somersault in my belly as the chair swung up and away, defying gravity. The show grounds would shrink by degrees. "Look over there, Mia," my grandparents would cheer at the top, as a cool breeze lapped at my face and hair. Then we'd descend and rejoin the heady scents of oils and sugars, picking out individual voices over the thrum. I remember the Ferris wheel as an endless tide of rising and falling, pulling out, zooming in. "Can we go again?" I'd ask at the disappointing stillness. And we would. What wouldn't my grandparents have done for me? They'd spend whole days indulging my whims, then idle the car in the driveway to kiss me goodbye.

"Be a good girl, Mia," Grandma would say. I'd watch the car recede until the cul-de-sac was quiet. Only then would my mother open the door.

I used to think it was normal for women to hate their parents, to hold grudges and keep doors closed to them. So I wasn't surprised to discover I hated mine, or to learn she hated me back. Every word was a criticism. It was easier to shut her out than to let her awful voice in.

Kewpie dolls stare blankly at me from a stall. They haven't changed a bit, though my grandparents are dead and I'm no longer a little girl.

I take a breath and fall into the slipstream, not thinking, following. I bustle into steamy pavilions with free tastings, and come out the other end, greeted by carnies trying to coax me. *Everyone's a winner!* I'm drawn along with the crowds, between bumper cars and ghost trains.

Everyone bustles about me, around me, and I'm kind of glad the Royal Show is happening, the way it always has, with people wasting money on short-lived rides, eating food they'll regret later. It's good to be surrounded by color and noise, despite the threat of cancer and the sadness of what's been taken. Perhaps others here have lost something too. Or, worse, lost someone. Are yet to lose someone. Of these thousands of people, one in every two will get cancer. One in five will die of it. And somehow they still manage to slam bumper cars into one another and laugh at themselves in magic mirrors.

That's where I see him.

Rhys makes faces in front of a magic mirror. A pretty girl's beside him, a purple monkey on her shoulders.

It sticks me to the spot. I haven't thought of him in weeks. I want to throw up.

The two of them experiment laughingly with poses. He's wearing a hat I haven't seen. The girl's familiar—I think she was a year below me at school.

Then he guides her away, still showing off to make her laugh, which she does. I follow at a distance, watching the way he hooks a finger in the back of her jeans pocket, the way he used to with me. He pays for tickets for the Wipeout, though I know he's scared of heights. As they wait in the line, I see he's using his old routine, angling his head when he listens, making her believe she's everything. The hat's the only new thing about him. The girl smiles and twists, cute in her short shorts and crocheted top. She plays with the golden half-a-heart on a necklace. When he kisses her I turn away.

Half a heart isn't good enough, Rhys. She'll realize too, eventually, when she outgrows those shorts, and the monkey, and you.

I walk through alleyways, where laughing clowns shake their heads at me from either side. *Don't cry,* they say. *Don't you dare cry.*

And if it wasn't for Zac's postcard in my pocket, I probably would.

• • •

There are hundreds of pens in the alpaca pavilion, but eventually I find Sheba's. She looks at me with her big eyes, as if to say, *Oh, it's you. Get me out of here, would you?*

She's the worst behaved through the judging, resisting when the judge checks her teeth and wool. She needs the familiar smell of Bec to soothe her. I watch nervously, surrounded by spectators young and old who've come for this strange ceremony. The old judge bends and leans, crouches and appraises. He's quick at dodging Sheba's kick. Spectators tut.

I take photos with my phone as Sheba's escorted, ribbonless, back to her pen.

I hadn't realized how many alpaca farms exist, or how many types of sheep they pack into the shearing and wool pavilion: poll Dorsets, white Suffolks, Suffolks, and white Dorpers. Farmers in flannel and denim discuss market prices. Some of the young ones remind me of Zac—the way he would lean on a fence as if it were put there for his thinking.

God, I wish he was here, but I know he has a trip-of-a-lifetime to make the most of. I buy him a Freddo Frog show bag. On the train home, I reread the postcard, just to hear his voice.

Funny. I never pegged him as the Disneyland type.

35
Mia

Six days later an envelope arrives from America. Inside are two things: a postcard from Zac and a recipe in Wendy's looping letters.

Howdy Mia

We're in San Fran, home of the Chinese fortune cookie, jeans, Irish coffee, and more weirdos than anywhere else. Celebrity spot #3: Robin Williams eating a bagel. True! How lucky's that?

How was Sheba? Did Miriam scoop the cake prizes? Mum's writing out the recipe if you promise to "guard it with your life"!! Lucky you, ha ha.

Disneyland tomorrow. Any requests for souvenirs? Or should I guess your favorite character . . . Snow White? Dad has this thing about imitating Mickey Mouse: high pants, big gut, squeaky voice. Evan's got a lifelong crush on Pocahontas, which he better keep under control.

Mum's itching for her 2pm Starbucks.
Wish me luck
Zac

Imagining Zac in San Francisco isn't easy. There'll be no crowing roosters to wake him. No heavy wellies or long pink gloves.

I reread the letter on the bus to the amputee clinic, where I'll be getting my leg adjusted. I read it again, counting the references to "luck." It's typical of him to use the word so casually.

And he's not the only one. During chemo, doctors would use it around my mum—they knew better than to try it on me. *Lucky we've caught it at this stage. Lucky it's isolated.* And then, after surgery, I'd overhear nurses in the corridor. *She doesn't realize how lucky she is.*

In the clinic waiting room, there's a girl a bit younger than me. Her bandaged stump is mid-thigh. I catch her looking at mine with envy. *Below knee,* I see her thinking jealously. *Lucky.* She wears a wig and I remember how mine irritated me.

I have to look away. Does she really think I'm *lucky?*

It was bad luck that gave me cancer in the first place, wasn't it? Bad luck put me through hell. So how can it suddenly be *good luck* to survive with this much intact? Am I lucky to walk without much of a sway?

It's impossible, this luck business. I wish it would just piss off and let me make my own mistakes. I want control back over my life.

I want to bake a fruit cake.

And then? I want to do something else, like get a job or

travel. I can't afford to fly to America, but I can go to towns I've never been, where people don't know me. I want to look at a place with fresh eyes, the way Zac does.

At home, I lie in the small pool in the courtyard and admire the olive tree. When Zac's back, I'll invite him to Perth and the two of us can squeeze in here together. We can eat fruit cake and drink iced coffees, and he can tell me all about Disneyland.

"Ariel," I say aloud, remembering my favorite character. As a girl, I was obsessed with Ariel from *The Little Mermaid*, with her beautiful red hair and shimmering tail.

I still have the DVD, so I go inside to play it. I know each song by heart.

But the movie's not the same as it used to be. Ten years ago, I thought Ariel was incredibly romantic, sacrificing her tail for two legs to be with a human she loved. I'd forgotten how the witch stole her voice, and how she suffered in silence to walk.

What a crappy swap, I think. *Keep the tail*, I'd tell Ariel now.

Keep the tail and sing.

• • •

Hey there Mia
Start spreading the neeewws . . .
Why do they call NYC the Big Apple? New Yorkers eat nothing but pretzels, kebabs, and black "cawfee." Mum's discovered so-called fat-free chocolate brownies and she's testing the claim.

I keep expecting Jerry and Elaine to step out of a diner. We're doing a Seinfeld tour tomorrow, so anything's possible. Mum even bought me a Seinfeld trivia game, which is hilarious. You better get cramming cuz when I'm back, I'm going to kick your butt. (I've got dibs on George.)

Gotta go.

Zac

PS. I've also heard a rumor Emma Watson's in town . . . just sayin'.

Zac's letters are falling into a comforting pattern. I love the commentary and the random challenge he gives me each time. I know he's just trying to keep me busy. It's working.

Whenever the phone rings, I still hope it's him. Maybe it's three a.m. and he's lonely in the city that never sleeps.

This morning, Mum beats me to the landline. She answers a few questions, confused, then covers the mouthpiece.

"It's someone from the amputee clinic. They want you to come in."

"Why?" I was there only two weeks ago for an adjustment.

"A fitting, they say. For your new leg."

"I've got it," I remind her, tapping the molded fiberglass. This one should last me a few years. "It was probably meant for the other girl," I say, remembering the way she looked at me.

Mum hangs up the phone. "Strange. They said it was a carbon-fiber one. For you."

• • •

It's in the DVD store that I notice it. A strange feeling in my chest.

At first it reminds me of the butterflies that I used to experience on the Ferris wheel. But I'm standing on solid ground so there's no reason for it.

I scan the TV series lined alphabetically along the shelves. Many of them are set in New York. I flip them over, browsing the front and back covers. New York streets have become familiar to me through sitcoms and dramas like these — the yellow cabs, the wide sidewalks, the narrow apartment buildings. Even the New York City skyline is recognizable.

Ideas are born this way: a convergence of two unrelated things. The first: a *Friends* DVD case. The second: the memory of a postcard. Two images come together like strangers in a doorway. They jostle, apologize, and sidestep, but still . . . something happens.

Something flutters in my chest.

Back at home, I watch episodes of *Seinfeld* as if I'm looking for Zac. Why is it suddenly so hard to picture him there?

I reread his postcards and letter. There's no doubt it's his handwriting. It's Zac's style, too. His careless talk of celebrities. Weather. His mum's obsession with Starbucks.

But now that I think about it, that feels odd too. On the few times I'd spoken to Wendy, she'd always offered me tea.

I run my fingers over the right corner of an envelope. There's an airmail sticker and a blue $2.20 stamp of the New York City skyline. It's the old skyline, complete with the Twin Towers.

It's been more than a decade since the World Trade Center

fell. It makes me wonder why the buildings would still be featured on stamps when even old *Friends* DVD covers have been updated to a skyline without the towers. Why would a country risk opening old wounds?

What I feel isn't dread. Dread is an anchor in your gut. Dread is losing your hair, dropping out of school, waking up without a leg and wishing you'd died. Dread is heavy and it holds you down.

What I feel is up higher, in my rib cage. It's more like the stirring of fear and I don't know why. I've been through so much already. What could possibly still scare me?

I check Zac's other postcards, with stamps proclaiming "Los Angeles" and "San Francisco." Is it odd that none of them have dates? Is it coincidence the postmarked circles end at the stamp? That the corners peel off too easily, as if they've been peeled off before?

I have no reason to believe that Zac is anywhere but New York, doing all the things he tells me.

But giant wings beat at my heart and I know.

I know.

I know I'm being had.

36
Mia

I ring the number from the website.

"The Good Olive, olive oil and petting farm."

"Bec?"

"Yes."

"You're there."

"Yes . . . who is this?"

"You're back?"

"Back from where?"

I hang up.

I try Zac's cell but it goes to voice mail. I sense him watching it; letting it. Does he know I know?

The wings have become a panicked bird in my chest. Nothing helps: the air in the courtyard, the tree with five green olives. Its kind, calming leaves. So many mixed messages.

"The Good Oli—"

"Bec."

"Who is this?"

"Is Zac there?"

Silence.

"Mia?"

"Is he?"

A goat bleats in the distance. A cackle of chickens.

"But he told me—"

"I know."

My voice crumbles. "Why would he say that?"

What an awful person I must be to make him go to such lengths—fake letters, old stamps, all those American clichés—just to avoid me. His whole family must be in on the joke, laughing at my gullibility. My ugliness.

"Mia," says Bec. "Mia, he didn't—"

"He didn't have to *lie*. If he hates me that much—"

"He doesn't hate you."

How stupid I was for believing Zac could like me, when all his kindness was designed to get me to leave, to fuck off out of his life once and for all.

"Mia, I told him not to—"

"Because of my leg?"

"It's not your leg. It's nothing—"

"I won't bother him anymore."

"Mia, he's sick."

Everything stops but that word. It snaps off in the air. It drifts from the other words, sending ripples across the courtyard, rustling each leaf of the tree. Five olives hang their small heads.

In the ordinary world, "sick" means a cold. A headache. A sore throat. A complaint: *I'm sick of this. She makes me sick.*

But in our world it's something else.

I'd assumed he was still well. I'd figured he'd had his turn and survived unscathed, to live as ordinary people do with ordinary marrow. He was supposed to be the one giving me strength. To keep distracting me, reminding me how lucky I am.

It's not fair. I've been the lucky one all along—the ninety-eight percent—and I never deserved to be.

Zac?

And the bird rips free, screeching up and over the fence, already tearing south.

• • •

My own cancer was a dog at my ankle, refusing to let go. I'd thought that all cancers were like that, gripping fiercely at bone until cut free and disposed of. But they're not. Zac's wasn't.

I should have suspected something. He'd stopped updating Facebook, the way I once had. He withdrew into that dark place where you don't have to be strong or funny. I should've realized he was hiding, because I've hidden there before.

One website leads me to another as I track my way through help sites, forums, blogs, and online diaries. I had no idea there'd be so many. When I was sick, I thought I was the only one.

Who'd have thought you can empty a human of their blood and marrow and replace the whole lot, only to have cancer reappear months later.

Unlike my cancer, Zac's has nothing that can be cut out. Leukemia gets into the blood and lungs, heart and stomach. It's everything that makes him who he is — that boy who dared to knock, who'd rather make up lies than drag me down with his sadness. Even now, he wants to keep me safe.

Mum finds me in my dark room with the iPod on repeat. I don't know what the song is. It doesn't matter, as long as it's loud.

She stops at the door.

"Are you sore?" she says, but I shake my head and turn away. Why does it always have to be about my leg? There are worse things.

She's supposed to avoid me when I'm like this. My music is the signal to leave.

But tonight it draws her in. I recall something Bec had said once. *When an animal's kicking and fighting the most, that's the time you need to pull it closer.*

Mum pulls me close and I'm just a kid, terrified. She smoothes my hair as I tell her all about the boy from Room 1. The beautiful boy who put my pieces back together.

"He shouldn't have lied."

"He thought it was best."

"He should've told me."

"Everyone's doing their best, Mia."

"What do I do?"

"Get some sleep. We'll do something tomorrow."

She helps me into bed and squeezes my hands. When she leaves, she switches off the music and the light.

There's no sleeping. In the darkness, I read online tributes to children now dead. Children who still believed in Santa. I watch the videos of bald teens, bored in isolation like Zac must have been. I read the blogs of patients who fought the first time, fought again at relapse, then ran out of momentum at the third attempt, or fourth. How many times before they give in? How many times can they go through this?

How many times will Zac?

I force myself to ignore the sites with statistics, focusing instead on survivors' stories. I hope he reads them too.

I read about patients having four treatments. There are successes even then, even after the fifth. A woman has six bone marrow transplants over ten years and she lives, the blood of strangers coloring her cheeks. Twelve years in remission, thriving on a vegan diet. Others, too, who've fought so long and won, grateful to acupuncture, spirulina, wheatgrass, Vitamin B, yoga, and prayer.

I hope he's not out of fight.

It's three a.m. and my mind runs hot. I check Facebook, wanting him to be there, his green dot pulsing like a faraway star.

Of course it's not. I type a message anyway.

> Zac, you can't lie anymore. I know you're home. Bec told me

But the words look accusing. I remember how patient he was with me in the hospital.

I start again, slowly. I let the tears fall.

> Hi Zac.
>
> How's New York? Is it cold? Does steam really come up from the grates? Does it feel like a big movie set?
>
> I won't bore you with my news. Your life's way more exciting than mine.

When do you get home? I'm all out of pears, and could do with a decent grilled cheese. I can't seem to get it right. What's the secret?

It occurred to me that I haven't said thanks yet. So . . . thanks. You always knew what to say, or not say. Thanks for letting me stay at the farm, even though it got you in trouble. Thanks for worrying, and for not giving up on me. You didn't care about my leg or my hair (maybe a little bit about my hair . . .). You saw me for what I was, not what I wasn't. You made me imagine that life could go on. That I wanted it to.

If you get this message (if I don't chicken out and delete it first) can you reply? I know you're busy in New York stalking Emma Watson, but if you find yourself in an Internet café and get this email, please reply. I'd like to read your typos again ;-)

Love

Mia

PS. You always called me lucky and I'm beginning to think you might be right. I never thought I'd be lucky enough to have a friend like you. You're the nicest person to have ever knocked on my wall.

Typing this has taken all I have. I'm wrung out.

Before, everything I'd written had been about me—it's *always* been about me.

I need this message to be for him.

37
Mia

Mum finds me asleep over my laptop in the morning, my fingers still at the keyboard.

"Mia."

"Why didn't he tell me?"

"Come on, Mia. Come wash your face."

I stay in the bathroom as Mum phones the farm. I hear pieces of conversation but I can't make sense of it. "Bec says we're welcome to visit," she explains to me, after. "But she doesn't want us to . . . waste our time."

"What does Zac want?"

Mum shakes her head, not understanding. "Bec says he doesn't talk."

"At all?"

"He goes to school, but at home . . . no. Not about the relapse. Do you want to go, Mia?"

"I can't just show up."

"Do you want to?"

"Mum, he doesn't *want* me there."

"Don't guess what's inside his head, Mia. Think what's in your own." She holds my shoulders still. "What do you want to do?"

Me? It's a no-brainer. My whole body feels the pull of him.

• • •

Mum rings her work.

"Sorry, Donna, something's come up . . . No, Mia's fine. She's well." Mum smiles, and I see her relief in being able to say that. "She's good. Her hair's at her shoulders now. No, it's something else. I'll need a few days, okay?"

She cancels her date with the roses man—Ross, his name is—fielding the same lightning-quick questions. "No, she's well. My daughter's well."

I don't understand why people I've never met are jumping to these conclusions. What fears has my mum been sharing with them that she hasn't shared with me?

I follow her into the garage, where she tops up the car's water and oil, and checks the spare tire. She's never seemed afraid. Not to me. Irritated, yes. Pushy and controlling, definitely. But I never imagined she was scared of losing me.

And I was so keen on being lost.

She grabs a suitcase. We chuck some clothes in, then raid the kitchen for water bottles and snacks. Into the boot of the car she throws towels and blankets. She's efficient at escape—much better than I was.

She pulls up the garage door, then starts the car.

"Mia?"

I can't move.

"Mia, jump in."

Zac doesn't want me there. He just wants to drop out and I can't blame him. If it were me, I'd want to bolt to the Gold Coast and go out with a bang: parties, drugs, strangers in hotel rooms. Fuck the world and all its bad luck. Fuck doctors and needles and pain. Fuck Google and all its statistics because they don't mean a thing when it's *your* life they're talking about.

"Are you coming?"

"We can't fix him, you know."

"I know."

"We can't just turn up and fix him."

"Then we just turn up. Here."

She passes me an old map book. It gives me something to concentrate on as I navigate the best way through our suburb and the next, zigzagging our way to the turnoff for the Albany Highway. Here, the car starts to struggle as the road climbs up and away. The city shrinks in the rearview mirror.

"I don't want to go."

"I know."

I put the book away. We won't be turning off this road for another four hours.

"So it's back? His leukemia?"

Mum nods.

"When's he coming up to the hospital?" It's selfish of me, but if Zac came to Perth for treatment, I could visit him whenever I wanted, couldn't I?

Mum keeps her eyes on the road. "I'm not sure he is."

The highway dips and curves at speed. Suburbs segue into bushland; bushland turns to paddocks so green that it looks like carpet's been laid out for the lambs. Near and far, canola fields form bright yellow squares. The world looks honey-sweet out here, the trees pale and gentle.

But every now and then I notice thin shadows cast by birds and I know there's so much yet to be afraid of.

• • •

Near a town, we slow from seventy to fifty to thirty. We pass a few houses with stands selling fruit, then a real estate agency and chicken takeout place. It feels familiar, though it's not until we pull into the service station that I remember. This is where I told the guy I was a shark victim. Where Zac and I bought corn dogs and ate them in the sun.

Mum fills up the gas tank.

"Do you know what a corn dog is?" I ask her.

"Of course. I used to work here."

"*Here?*"

I look around. There's nothing but the service station and its gas pumps. Next door is a brick factory and, across the road, an orchard.

"It wasn't self-serve then. We had to fill the cars for them."

"Since when did you work at a service station?"

"Since my parents owned it."

"This?"

"I grew up here. Our house was around the back."

"Why didn't you ever tell me that?"

"I did."

Even if she had, I wouldn't have remembered. History and geography were always my least favorite topics.

The fuel pump chugs and Mum stares at the columns as they *tick-tick-tick*. I wonder how many times she's leaned against cars, watching the numbers flick over.

"This is where I met your father."

I push myself off the car to examine the gas pump in all its dirty, smelly significance. *This* is the starting point of my life? At pump number two, unleaded?

"I said I *met* him here," Mum clarifies. "You were conceived about twenty k's that way. Weeks later. By a river."

"Gross."

"You asked."

"No, I didn't. Who was he?"

"I've told you."

"Tell me again."

"Chris. A salesman from Perth. I put twenty dollars in his Magna. His window was down and he was playing Silverchair. He caught me singing along as I leaned across his windscreen. He even gave me a dollar tip."

"What color was the car?"

"Red."

"Was he tall?"

"Why does that matter?"

"'Cause I'm taller than you. Was he?"

"Not overly. No, not really."

"Did he ask for your number?"

"We didn't have cell phones, Mia. He came back the next

week to fill up, over there." Mum points to pump number three. "He was playing Powderfinger then."

"And then?"

"He kept coming back."

"You liked him?"

Mum releases the trigger and the ticking stops. She hangs up the nozzle, screws on the gas cap, and blinks slowly at the pump as if it's him, eighteen years ago.

"I thought he would be my ticket out of here."

"Was he?"

"You were, Mia."

•   •   •

We leave the service station and coast through the main street of town. We pass a burger place, a supermarket, butcher, news-agent, and park. There's a sign for a school and a hospital. There are rows of houses behind the highway. It's a community, I guess, but not one I'd want to live in.

I try to imagine Mum as a schoolgirl laughing with friends in the park, telling them about the man in the Magna who's so much more sophisticated than the local boys. I picture her in a short uniform, drinking Coke through a straw, enjoying the word *sophisticated*.

On each corner I see ghosts of her. Mum drives slowly, as if she sees them too.

She slows the car even more, then parks in front of a bak-ery. I follow her lead up the pavement and through plastic strips that create a kind of door. The place stinks of yeast.

"It's changed." Mum frowns, disappointed. "There used to

be long trays of jam doughnuts there." The doughnuts on the shelves are small and iced with sprinkles. I wouldn't mind one, but Mum orders us something else.

"We used to sit at a table in the corner and eat cream puffs every day after school."

"And you weren't a fatty?"

"Bonnie was like a stick and Clare was . . . voluptuous . . . in all the right places."

I carry the cream puffs and iced coffees to a table, then push crumbs off the plastic tablecloth.

"Don't you want to get going?"

I shake my head—there's no rush. Whatever time we arrive at Zac's house, the outcome will be the same. If I'm honest, I don't want to go at all.

Mum tears the bag open. "They're not the same."

"What about you? What were you like?"

"I was . . . normal."

"Normal, my ass," I laugh, as Shay's words come back to me. "Did you like school?"

"It beat working at the gas station."

"Favorite subject?"

"Biology."

"Weird. What did you wear to your formal?" For some reason I imagine Mum in blue velvet, a huge flower in her hair.

"I didn't go, Mia. I left to have you."

So there was no blue velvet dress, just a pregnant teenager in a car with her parents. The three of them headed to Perth, where no one would know Mum's shame. The three of them would start again. The four of us.

"What happened to the Magna man?"

"Mia, I've told you this."

"No, you haven't. Tell me now."

She's prodding the cream puff with a fork. She doesn't take her eyes off it. "He said he'd take me away with him, but he didn't. He never came back."

I imagine a ghost of Mum still at the service station. Waiting. Growing fat with her secret. Heartbroken and helpless. Watching the road. Falling apart.

"Where were Bonnie and Clare?"

"They didn't know. I didn't tell them, even when I left."

"Why not?"

"I was humiliated."

"Because of me?"

"Because I'd talked up this fantasy life with this fantasy man, and it never happened."

I see my mum as this: an accumulation of cream puffs and Cokes, memorized song lyrics and dreams of a better life, somewhere far away. I see her as a teenager who just wants to be loved, who, like me, would rather hide than let people see who she really is: imperfect and ashamed. Not winning, losing. Afraid. Running.

Why do we run?

"Don't you miss your friends?"

"It's ancient history. I should've got a doughnut."

"Do you regret having me?"

"No, Mia. I told you that already." If she did, I wouldn't know. From the time she forced me to get braces in primary school, I've blocked out most of what she told me. *It's so you don't have crooked teeth like mine!* Six months of arguing, and I lost. I've been fighting her instructions since. *Iron your clothes. Do your homework. Pull your shoulders back. Stay in school. Don't see that boy.*

I blocked it all out. And then: *Amputate the leg. Save my girl.*

I didn't know she was saying she loved me.

"Tell me again."

• • •

A paper bag with two jam doughnuts vibrates on the dashboard. The town is long behind us when Mum swears suddenly.

"Did I pay for the fuel?"

I think back to the gas station: Mum leaning on the car; Mum talking to the pump.

I laugh. "No."

"Shit."

She bites her lip and looks at me, but doesn't turn the car around. "We can always stop on the way home . . ."

We both know it won't happen. Neither of us wants to go back.

A quick memory makes me suck in air.

"What?"

"The corn dog," I say. "I was the one who dared Zac to eat it. That could've made him sick."

"No, Mia."

"He had a whole list of things he couldn't eat. We didn't know what was *in* it. He shouldn't have . . ."

Mum puts a hand on my thigh. "Mia, the corn dog didn't make him sick."

My tears splash the back of her hand. "But what if it did?"
"It didn't."
"What if it was me?"
"It wasn't."
"He's my friend," I say. My best friend.
"Then don't let him go."

38
Mia

Sheep glance in our direction, then bow their heads to nip again at grass. Dusk dilutes the sky. Mum turns off the engine.

THE GOOD OLIVE! OLIVE OIL AND PETTING FARM. An arrow points the way to the entrance. After that, another will point to the store, the sheep, and the alpacas. Then there'll be the sign that says NO ENTRY — RESIDENCE. And beyond, a house. Inside, a bedroom with orange curtains.

But I'm not going anywhere. I'm dead tired. My limbs wouldn't move even if I wanted them to.

"Mia."

"Go without me."

I wish I could be on a bus, leaving this behind. Or a plane, up and away, above all this, where life is simple.

Mum turns on the radio. *Shhh*, it says, as it searches for a frequency. *Shhh*. The song it settles on is quiet and acoustic, the kind Bec would hum to as she painted. The kind that makes me cry regardless of the words.

I'm not brave enough. What good am I to Zac if I lose it over a stupid song?

Mum rubs my back again. She cries too. She's not brave enough either.

The last of the daylight dissipates. In the grainy shadows, I see a guy letting himself into a pen. He drops feed at his feet, where goats crowd him.

He's older than Zac, I think, with fairer hair. Evan? I'd only met him once.

He pushes away a goat and wipes at tears with the back of his sleeve. *Oh god,* I think, *he's not brave enough either.*

• • •

Bec's the one who greets us at her house, her blond hair longer than before. Some of it's clutched in a baby's fist. She kisses me on a cheek and tells me I look good.

"This is Stu," she says, waving one of the baby's chubby arms. I shake his hand. He has Zac's eyes, though they're more blue than gray.

"He's cute."

"I did make a cute one, eh?"

She takes Mum through to the spare room, where they put the suitcase.

"Do you want to hold him?"

I hear Mum fuss over the baby, the way she's supposed to. She asks how old he is, how long he is, how he sleeps, what he does with his hands. She jigs him as they walk to Stu's room.

I stay in the living room: it's the wood fire that mesmerizes me. It whips and licks, devouring everything in its reach. It pushes against the glass, angry at being contained.

From the baby's room, Bec lowers her voice, but not enough. "The first time, he was strong . . . the second time, even stronger . . ." Bec's whispers aren't meant for me. "But this time . . . he's given up."

"What do you mean?" Mum doesn't know the way sickness wraps around you. How it'll crush you if you let it.

"He's broken."

If they could, these flames would smash the glass and lash across the floorboards, eating up the furniture and the walls and me.

"You must be Mia."

The voice startles me. I stand up but can't see the man. Flares are bright in my eyes.

"So you're the one who caused all that pain—"

"What?" I shake my head, trying to clear my vision.

"Bec still complains about that leg wax. She says it was worse than childbirth. You did a good job on her eyes, though."

I see the shape of Anton, but can't make out his face.

"Did I go overboard with the fire?"

"Maybe."

"They're putting the bub to sleep. You want a soda?"

"No, thanks."

"Tea?"

"No, I'm fine."

"How long are you staying?"

I blink, willing the flares to shrink behind my eyelids.

"I don't know . . . I don't think I am."

"It's good you've come," he says, but I shake my head again, not believing him. "Bec's glad you're here. And Wendy." He leans against the wall. His hair is blond, I notice. His skin is tanned. He has a kind face. "You *are* Mia, aren't you?"

"Yeah."

"The real Mia? The one Zac named the baby alpaca after?"

I check him for sincerity and he nods — there's no reason for him to lie.

I close my eyes again, wood cracking in my skull, stars detonating in my eyes.

• • •

In the main house, Zac's mum hugs me quickly and ushers us through the hallway, where family photos smile down at us from angles. She admires my hair and introduces herself to Mum. "I'm Wendy."

We stand awkwardly near the table that's been set for five. I add up numbers in my head and Wendy catches me. "He won't be joining us."

She takes us through to the kitchen, saying that the men will be back soon. The counter is a mess of boards and knives.

"You haven't eaten, have you?" She looks at the clock.

"No."

"I know it's late but . . . I got caught up packing boxes. Evan's feeding and Greg's been at the dam, I think. They'll be back soon." She checks the time again. "Do you like lamb?"

The kettle screams and Wendy lunges for it.

Mum helps Wendy with the tea. *English breakfast or Earl*

Grey? Milk? I don't care. Wendy digs through cupboards for matching saucers.

Outside the kitchen window, Bec's standing in the dark, hanging diapers on the clothesline. I can see Evan by the hayshed, with a flashlight and a bucket. Farther out, I notice headlights dipping beside a fence line, heading this way. They're not a family, they're fragments. Wendy rattles a teacup beside me.

"Tea? You must be tired, after the drive." Soon the dining room will be crowded with food and small talk and noise, and everyone will avoid the Zac-size hole that's opened up between them.

"Here you are, Mia. Sugar?"

But I'm sick of pretending. A Zac-size hole can't be filled with anything but Zac.

The hallway is long and quiet. It leads to four bedrooms. The doors are closed. I pass one, two. I tread the soft carpet. I feel the pull of him. Three. The world drops away behind me.

I press my palm against the end door. A door is all that's between us. *Zac?* I can't summon a single word.

Knock.

It's all I can do. I tilt into his door, where sadness is a spell sealing him inside.

Knock.

I think he knows it's me. I lean an ear closer, in case there's a *tap*.

I don't know how it must feel for your body to turn against you again and again. To spend months fighting death, to win then lose, win then lose, then have to put the armor back on. To calculate the odds. Recalculate. *Forget the math,* I want to tell him.

"Zac," I say.

"Shhh."

His voice is closer than I expected.

"Zac?"

"I'm writing you a postcard."

"From where?"

"Boston."

"What's it like?"

"It's snowing."

"Yeah?" I slide to a crouch so I'm closer to the voice. "What else?"

"Did you know the Old Hancock Tower flashes red when a Red Sox game has been rained out?"

"I didn't know that." I don't care if he's plagiarizing Wikipedia. Is his make-believe such a bad thing? "Seen any celebrities?"

"Not yet."

"Can I read it?"

"When it's done."

"I'll wait," I say. And I do, leaning in to the door that separates his world from this one. I picture him in Boston, getting lost in the city with his family. Tracking down warm restaurants. He's making snow angels with Bec. He's running away from Evan's snow missiles, laughing and dodging like a half-forward flank is supposed to.

Then I'm being lifted in a man's arms and carried down the hallway, through a doorway, and outside to Bec's house. When did it get so cold?

Then I'm in Bec's spare room again, being eased onto the soft bed. Mum's above me. So are Wendy, Bec, and Anton.

"Are you hungry?" Mum asks.

"No."

Mum rolls up my jeans and unclips the prosthetic from me. Her fingers worry at the clasp. Evan lingers near the door, watching.

Mum tells me it's okay. That I should go back to sleep.

"Sorry," I say to Wendy. "He's in Boston."

I'm not the answer they were hoping for.

39
Mia

Outside the window, there are too many stars in the sky.

It takes a while to remember where I am: at Zac's farm, in Bec's spare bed, my fiberglass leg by the wall. For the first time, I'm actually glad to see it. I can reach over, pull it on, climb out of the window, and hit the ground smoothly.

Three a.m.

Wet grass scrunches beneath me. I creep toward the main house and step up to Zac's window. It's half open, orange curtains gesturing me inside. I want to crawl through and slip into his bed, where he'll shuffle across to make room. Moonlight will polish his pale skin, gentle on the purple scar below his collarbone. He'll share his pillow and pull the blanket across us. He'll tell me I've gone up to a ten, that I'm too good for a six like him. Maybe I'll tell him what he really is. Maybe I won't.

"Zac?"

But his room is empty, and a breeze tickles the hair at my neck.

• • •

I find him where I first found him that day I'd followed Bec and the tour group. He'd had his back to us then, standing by the far gate. I remember how my wound throbbed with pain and how I'd wanted to blame him for this, for lying to me. He'd promised I was going to be okay, and I wasn't.

Even then he was somewhere else. I saw he was vulnerable. That's when I knew I could trust him.

Now, he's a flannel ghost in the moonlight. He sits on the fence, his bare feet hooked into the wire rungs below.

"Stop." Zac straightens an arm and I freeze.

"What?"

"You'll scare her."

Her? There's nothing here but us, a fence, and a dark forest. Zac was always the rational one, but who knows what cancer can do to a person? What it could be doing to him now?

I try to keep my voice steady. "Zac. There's no one—"

"Shhh."

My chest hurts. I can't cry now.

Then two amber eyes glint from the darkness.

Zac warns, "Be still."

"Is it a fox?"

"Shhh."

She's beautiful and she knows it. I sense her confidence and poise. I think she's judging me.

The eyeballs shift, skimming behind branches, and I catch glimpses of her—a pointed ear, fur, a foot—as she slinks fluidly through trees. I envy her grace. I resent the pull she has over Zac—enough to draw him from a warm bed to sit on a fence in the nighttime.

The creature pads to a stop, licks at her leg, and returns her gaze to Zac. I see they know each other. I sense I'm intruding.

But I've come all this way for a reason.

I take two steps forward, even when Zac shakes his hand at me. I take three more to reach him, even though he tells me not to. The oval eyes watch me as I put one hand on his leg and wrap the other around his arm, holding on.

"It's cold, Zac. Come back inside."

His arm jerks but I tighten my grip. Somewhere beneath his flannel pajamas, beneath skin and muscle and bone, too many abnormal white blood cells are reproducing. They're multiplying, trying to outnumber the healthy ones. I can't blame him for this.

"Tell me again about falling into a vat of Emma Watsons when you're a hundred."

He tries to elbow me away, but I draw closer.

"At least a vat of beer when you're ninety."

Zac twists free, so I pull myself up to the fence to join him. I grip my hands around the wooden railing to keep steady, not trusting my balance. He doesn't move across for me.

When I look up to the sky my breath comes out as milky puffs. They sail a bit and dissolve.

"Did you see that?" I point. "A burning meteorite." It's a lie, but the best one I can think of. "We should make a wish."

"I already did."

"I don't mean Disneyland. Go on, make a real wish."

"I wish you'd get off my fence."

I laugh. Even when he's mean he can be funny. "I like your fence. I like your farm."

"They asked you to come?"

"I wanted to."

"I didn't want you to."

"You're my friend, Zac."

He flinches and I don't blame him. He doesn't want a friend. He wants me to disappear, to fall off one edge of the world so he can fall off the other.

"Go home, Mia."

"But I just got here."

"Walk away."

"Sorry, I can't."

"You can, you've told me. Just stand up—"

"You haven't seen it yet, have you?" I roll my jeans up to my knee. "The socket's porous laminate. It's not the full spec, but it's better than the temp one, and yeah, as you say, I can walk. I could probably run, if I really had to. If something was chasing me."

I hold myself steady, then pull my knee closer.

"Admittedly it'd have to be something *slow* chasing me. The paralympians have special blades for speed. But it's light. Check it out."

He ignores me, so I roll down the liner, unclip it, and pull the prosthetic free.

"Feel it, go on. How often does a girl tell you to feel her leg?"

He inhales, saying my name on the outward breath. "Mia . . ."

"Sorry, that was lame. Actually, can I even say that now?"

His body tenses, preparing to slip off the fence and walk away. Desperate, I use the only weapon I have: I bend my arm back and pitch the prosthetic as high and hard as it will go. The thing flies end over end, skimming unseen leaves before thumping a tree in the bushland. Somewhere, the fox flees.

Zac gapes at me. "That was the *dumbest* thing."

The dumbest thing? It makes me laugh out loud. What I do next—sliding over the fence and hopping forward in the dark—is dumber by far. My jeans leg hangs low, snagging on prickly bushes. There would be snakes in this grass. Tree roots to stumble over and all kinds of holes to fall into. It's a minefield for a girl with one leg.

"What are you doing?"

"Looking for my leg."

"You won't find it."

"Did it go this way? I didn't see—"

"Stop! For fuck's sake, just *stop*."

I hop around on the spot, trying to keep my balance. When I see him from the front it wipes the smile from me. He's not the same Zac. The moon spills over his pale face, and I see he's more vulnerable than ever. I miss him.

"Leave me alone."

"I can't."

"Go home."

"I literally can't, *now*."

"Fuck. I don't need this."

"I'm not here to annoy you."

"Then why are you here?"

Without the fox, all his attention is on me. It's terrifying.

"I couldn't sleep."

"Why did you *come?* Who called you?"

"No one. I wanted a bath. And a pear."

"The fox can smell it."

"Pears?"

"Death," he says. "Can't you?"

"Zac—"

"I smell it."

"You can't."

"I should be dead."

"No, you shouldn't."

"If I were a rabbit or a chicken, I'd be dead already. If I were a sheep, I'd be shot."

"You're not a sheep, Zac."

"If I were a kid in Africa, I'd be long dead."

"You wouldn't," I say, though he might be right.

"I should be dead many times over."

"You're not in Africa," I remind him quietly. "You're Zac Meier, living in Australia. Your marrow sucks but you can fix it."

"You're an expert now?"

I lose my balance a bit, so I hop to a nearby branch and grab on.

"No, but I know you can get more chemo or another bone marrow transplant. As many as you need. Or you can try stem cord treatment. The results are promising."

"Is that so?"

"And there are drug trials all the time. New discoveries in Europe and America. There are plenty of options—"

"They're not options, Mia, they're time fillers."

"Then *fill . . . time!*" My voice rips at the dark. I'm so angry at him. I'm so angry *for* him. Suddenly I'm so seized with rage, I could hurl it at him and knock him off that fence. "Fill time until they *fix* you!"

"Everyone dies, Mia."

"But not everyone has a *choice*. That woman who fell in the vat of tomato sauce didn't. She fell in, and even in her last seconds, I bet she fought."

"She would've died anyway."

"Cam would've fought, if he had a choice." Zac winces at the name, so I go on. "If someone had offered Cam two options—to have a heart attack in his car or another round of treatment—he would've picked treatment, just in case, because who knew, it might just have worked and given him forty more years to surf and play pool and—"

"Cam only had ten percent."

"Fuck, if I had a ten percent chance of winning the Lotto, I'd put everything I had on it. Wouldn't you?"

"I'm not a gambler."

I know this already. If he were, we wouldn't be having this conversation. Zac's looked at the cards in his hand and tossed them in. I can't argue with that. Zac's decisions are formulated by logic and math, while mine are just whipped up by emotion and impulse and *I want, I want.*

I know I feel too much. I know I get carried away. But *I want, I want* Zac to live. To want to live. I *need* him to live, because I don't want to be in this world without him.

Emotion wins and, damn it, I cry. I close my eyes and hold tight to the branch as my grief spills free.

"Oh, for fuck's sake."

I hear my hacking sobs. Hear his contempt.

"Can't a guy sit on a fence without a fucking lecture? This isn't about *you*, Mia."

"I know."

"We're all going to die sooner or later."

"Then *later*, choose later! If Cam had a choice—"

"Cam's in Indonesia by now."

"He's not! He's—"

"What? In heaven? Playing pool with Elvis?"

I close my eyes and squeeze the branch as if it's everything. My hands cramp and my arms shake, and it comes to me now what courage is. Courage is standing still even though you want to run. Courage is planting yourself and turning toward the thing that scares you, whether it's your leg or your friends or the guy who could break your heart again. It's opening your eyes and staring that fear down.

I open my eyes. The night isn't as dark as it was.

"He's here," I say. "Cam's here."

I see the glassy bark of banksias and the glisten of ghost gums. I see those sharp shining dots above Zac's head, reminding me of the glow-in-the dark star that kept watch over me.

"He's everywhere," I say. And I know it's true.

"Cam died on a Saturday. Do you know how many other people died that day?"

I shake my head.

"Thirty-nine in Western Australia. Four hundred and three across the country."

"How do you know that?"

"Across the world, around one hundred and sixty thousand people died that day. One hundred and eleven each minute."

"You don't—"

"In the history of the world, how many people do you think have died?"

"I wouldn't know."

"Guess."

"No!"

"I don't know either, but it would be a whole shitload of burials and burnings and floating down the Ganges. So if every single person in the history of the world is currently hovering in the air around us, how the hell do we even breathe?"

It's not easy, I think, forcing myself to inhale, each breath reminding me I'm not alone. Cam's here. My grandma and grandpa are here. The ghosts of everyone who matters are with me, and in me. In my hands, the branch quivers with infinite pasts.

"What if you and Cam could somehow swap places for a day? If tomorrow you could be the ashes and Cam could be you, an eighteen-year-old guy with dodgy marrow. I know it's unscientific," I say, getting it in first, "and we're not in Disneyland, but just shut up and let me talk. What if Cam could wake up tomorrow and have a whole day?"

"As me?"

"As you, Zac Meier. What do you reckon Cam would do?"

Zac hooks his feet around the wire. He doesn't answer right away.

"Twenty-four hours in your body. What do you think?"

Zac's eyes are climbing the bark of the tree. Up and up, tracing the highest branch, then up above that. I don't know if he's listening or not, but I go on.

"He wouldn't muck around with a fucking calculator, I tell

you that. He'd take your one day, and he'd do everything he could. He'd fish and surf and eat cheddar cheese shish kebabs. He'd laugh and do handstands, and he'd probably even kiss me. He'd do everything he felt like doing, because you only get one life, Zac. One chance. And anyone who gives that up too easy—"

"It's not easy—"

"Is giving in, and giving in is a *stupid* way to die. Stupider than falling into a vat, or watering a fake Christmas tree with its lights on."

"Mia, shut up." Zac is coming toward me.

"And Cam would *never* pick a stupid way to die. He'd rather die trying than—"

Zac kisses me. I hate him. I love him.

Then he slides a hand over my mouth.

"Shut up and make a wish."

"Mm?"

"Shooting star. If you weren't crapping on so much you would've seen it. Make a wish."

My mouth clamped tight, tears flood me. One wish? Are you kidding? It's a no-brainer. And it's got nothing to do with my leg.

I say it in my head but I think he hears it, because he takes his hand away. Up close, I see the fear in him. If I could exchange places, I would.

He says, "I don't want to be stuck in that room again—"

"I know."

"I can't get Mum's hopes up."

"She's tough—"

"What if it doesn't work? What then?"

"Then you try again."

"How many times? How many trips?"

"I don't know."

"I just want to be normal."

"You are. You're still Zac. Sick or not. You're a nine out of ten."

"A nine?"

"Yeah. I'd give you a ten but you smell pretty bad. How long have you been in those pajamas?"

"I'm not afraid to die," he says.

I squeeze both his hands. "I know. But if you were, that'd be okay too."

"I'm not scared, I'm more . . . pissed off. You're supposed to do something in the world, like have kids or grow a forest. I haven't done anything like that. What's the point of me, other than leaving behind a messed-up family?"

"They want you to try again."

"They're not tough enough."

"They are."

"Are you?"

Shit, he's got me. I wipe my face quickly, then show him a flexed bicep, made strong by months on crutches. "What do you think?"

"That is pretty tough."

I balance myself against Zac's shoulders. I see how tired he is. I see how easy it would be to slip away. But I'm not going to let him, not after everything he's done for me. Maybe I'm just being selfish for wanting him around. Is that so wrong?

"I'm like the Hulk," I tell him.

"You turn green?"

"I'm tough," I promise. "Are you tough enough to piggyback me to Bec's house?"

"Why?"

"You can't expect me to hop all that way."

Zac swears and shakes his head. His eyes are gray. He's tired of me—tired of everything—but I grip him tight.

He says, "Do I have a choice?"

I shake my head back at him.

Zac turns and squats low for me. I hook my arms around his neck and make another wish.

Epilogue
Zac

From this side of the wall, I hear the newbie arrive. Nina goes through the instructions in her cheerful air hostess way, as if this flight will go smoothly.

It won't.

There'll be turbulence. Unexpected stopovers. Bad food. Loss of oxygen and moments of sheer panic.

But if the newbie's lucky, he won't endure it alone.

It sounds like a man in his fifties. I hear his questions. Later, there's the rattle of toiletries in the bedside drawer. He showers. Flicks through the TV channels.

I want to tell him not to order the chicken schnitzel on a Tuesday. That *Seinfeld* is the only show to watch while nauseous.

Mum is in the pink chair beside me with a magazine. "What's a nine-letter word for a precious stone?"

"Turquoise," Mia shouts, as if it's a competition. Which it kind of is.

They're supposed to take it in turns, these two, like fly-in, fly-out workers. Mum's here for one week, then Mia the next. They don't have to—I'm eighteen, for god's sake.

But sometimes their visits overlap. Mia arrives early and Mum's not so good at leaving.

"Go say hi to the newbie," I tell Mum, and she puts down her pen.

"Now?"

"Yeah."

"I could use a tea . . ."

When Nina comes to check on my IV lines, she ends up looking over Mia's shoulder, reading whatever chapter she's up to. In the hours I'm sleeping, Mia makes notes from her *Introduction to Nursing* textbook. After getting into university through special entry, she knows there'll be a tough ride ahead. Nina helps her sometimes, forgetting me altogether.

Tomorrow I'll be made new. I don't know who I'll be this time—a baby born in Bundaberg? Belgium? Brazil?—or even if the marrow will take graft and prosper. I'll need to get all my vaccinations done again. Around the world, more than 400,000 babies will be born tomorrow. Roughly five every second. There'll be all kinds of babies starting life from scratch, and then there'll be me.

At night, we watch the landing of Curiosity. From NASA's spacecraft, a robot vehicle the size of a small SUV is finally wheeling its way across the surface of Mars. Around Earth, scientists are cheering. Already they're analyzing data and recording the numbers of molecules, gases, humidity, minerals. They're probing, scraping, looking for life.

It gives me hope, in a way. If a robot can navigate its way 560 million kilometers through our solar system, then scientists can find a cure for something as boring as my white blood cells. They're closing in.

I don't turn on the iPad at night because Mia's beside me, sleeping in the pink chair. Every time I feel like I'm slipping off the edge of the Earth, she catches me. She has good hands. Her leg is good too, even better than the fiberglass one she'd showed me that night. Her new one has a flex foot and a silicone outer that looks like real flesh. She can run now, if she chooses to. Jump and dance if she wants. She can drive with it too.

Because why would I waste a Make-A-Wish grant on a trip to Disneyland? There are some wishes that money can buy, and then there's this: Mia without pain, walking in symmetry with a top-of-the-range, custom-made leg.

What wouldn't I do to keep the smile on her face? To hear that laugh, to have her fight with me, not against me. When we're together, there's no falling off, falling out, or falling down. I know there are no guarantees, but right now there's Mia, ten out of ten, more beautiful and surprising than ever.

And I am the luckiest.

Acknowledgments

I'd like to acknowledge the students I've had the privilege of working with on ward 3B over the past eight years. This novel is fiction, but it is inspired by you: your humor, courage, love, and beauty. A special mention to Tayla Hancock, whose belief in this story was with me at the beginning, and helped carry it through to the end. Thank you to her mother, Ros, for encouraging me to persevere.

I am grateful to friends who generously read early drafts: Ryan O'Neill (short story marvel and master of metaphor), Ruth Morgan (authority in youth, romance, and reason), Meg McKinlay (children's author and advocate for rhythm and melody), and Mum (tireless cheerleader). Suzanne Momber provided much enthusiasm and medical expertise, and kindly allowed me to exercise "creative license" when I needed to.

I'd like to thank Wendy Binks and her family for welcoming me into their homes and letting me loose in their petting farm, the Pentland Animal Farm, in Denmark. The experience was wonderful, and fed directly into the novel. Also, thank you to my teen neighbors, Jean and Will Morgan, for engaging in passionate debates about singers, video games, and vocab — you guys are hilarious, and priceless. Thanks to Ross and Wendy Morgan, who have witnessed the highs and lows of writing this novel. As always, you've been a rock.

Part of this novel was written in Adelaide in 2011, during a May Gibbs Creative Residential Fellowship. I appreciate the opportunity and heartfelt support given by the May Gibbs Literature Trust, and members of the Adelaide writing community.

Of course, this novel wouldn't be here without the incomparable Text. I am hugely grateful for the commitment and passion of the entire Text team. Special thanks go to Emily Booth, Chong, Imogen Stubbs, and my talented editors, Ali Arnold and Davina Bell. Thank you for believing in this book, and in me.